HG-12

APR - 4

Claws of the Eagle

Also by Andrew J. Fenady
in Large Print:

Double Eagles
The Man with Bogart's Face
The Rebel: Johnny Yuma

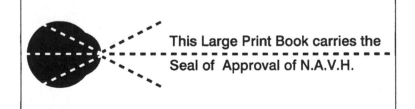

This Large Print Book carries the
Seal of Approval of N.A.V.H.

Claws of the Eagle

A Novel of Tom Horn and the Apache Kid

Andrew J. Fenady

Thorndike Press • Waterville, Maine

Published in 2004 by arrangement with
Arthur Pine Associates, Inc.

Thorndike Press® Large Print Western.

The tree indicium is a trademark of Thorndike Press.

The text of this Large Print edition is unabridged.
Other aspects of the book may vary from the original edition.

Set in 16 pt. Plantin by Myrna S. Raven.

Printed in the United States on permanent paper.

Library of Congress Cataloging-in-Publication Data

Fenady, Andrew J.
    Claws of the eagle : a novel of Tom Horn and the
Apache Kid / Andrew J. Fenady.
        p. cm.
    ISBN 0-7862-5933-7 (lg. print : hc : alk. paper)
    1. Horn, Tom, 1860–1903 — Fiction.   2. Apache
Indians — Wars, 1883–1886 — Fiction.   3. Scouts and
scouting — Fiction.   4. Large type books.   I. Title.
PS3556.E477C55 2003
813′.54—dc22   2003066290

For   John Wayne
             who knew and
             loved the west

and   Mary Frances
             who came with
             me to see
             the elephant

As the Founder/CEO of NAVH, the only national health agency solely devoted to those who, although not totally blind, have an eye disease which could lead to serious visual impairment, I am pleased to recognize Thorndike Press* as one of the leading publishers in the large print field.

Founded in 1954 in San Francisco to prepare large print textbooks for partially seeing children, NAVH became the pioneer and standard setting agency in the preparation of large type.

Today, those publishers who meet our standards carry the prestigious "Seal of Approval" indicating high quality large print. We are delighted that Thorndike Press is one of the publishers whose titles meet these standards. We are also pleased to recognize the significant contribution Thorndike Press is making in this important and growing field.

Lorraine H. Marchi, L.H.D.
Founder/CEO
NAVH

* Thorndike Press encompasses the following imprints: Thorndike, Wheeler, Walker and Large Print Press.

The Eagle

He clasps the crag with crooked hands;
Close to the sun in lonely lands.
Ringed with the azure world, he stands.

The wrinkled span beneath him crawls;
He watches from his mountain walls.
And like a thunderbolt he falls.

Alfred, Lord Tennyson

Chapter 1

The dawning sun jutted above the jagged mountain rim and flared into the big man's eyes, distorting his vision. His gnarled hand rubbed across his face. He blinked, squinted, and took another look toward the distant camp composed of two wickiups backed against the Rincon Range.

There was no visible sign of life, only dawn sounds, crickets and the chirps and chattering of hungry birds.

Al Sieber, chief of scouts, started to crawl forward. He was in his late fifties now, used up and juiced out. But enough of the old agility and a lot of the strength remained. Sieber had taken part in more Indian fights than Daniel Boone, Jim Bridger, and Kit Carson combined. His body had collected twenty-nine wounds.

Suddenly Sieber stiffened and froze. The bird noises had ceased.

A rifle barrel dipped and pointed just inches from the old scout's head. Sieber looked up the narrow, deadly rifle barrel to the man holding the Winchester. The man, dressed in a buckskin shirt and blanched brown pants, stretched up more than six feet, but from Sieber's position he looked about ten feet tall.

"Morning, Al." Tom Horn stood smiling out of a handsome catgut face with calm, silver blue eyes.

"Tom, you do know how to set up camp."

"Had a good teacher."

"Teacher needs to talk to you."

"Had breakfast, Al?"

"Yesterday."

"Well, let's have some breakfast and talk." Horn extended the butt of the Winchester to help Sieber. "How's the rheumatism?"

"Kicking up."

Tom Horn was a speck somewhere in the vast patchwork of Apachedom and Al Sieber had found him. But then Tom Horn had also found Al Sieber. For nearly a decade, the gruff, taciturn chief of scouts had been tutoring Tom Horn in the fine and bloody art of scouting and staying alive; now the two men nearly thought in tandem.

Part of it was inborn in Horn. Not everyone could be taught the rudiments of scouting. Not one in ten, or a hundred, or even a thousand. Not if the hunter's instinct was not there to begin with. That instinct was a part of Horn's mind and body. His eyes were made for the unseen trail and his hand for the trigger. But good eyes didn't necessarily make a good scout, and a single accurate shot didn't necessarily keep you alive in the warring world of Apacheria.

Sieber had honed Horn's natural abilities and perceptions. He had taught his eager pupil to accumulate and evaluate what had happened, what was happening, and what to do about it — with accuracy and alacrity. The two had saved each other's lives as casually as other men played cards.

More often than not, the stakes in the game Sieber and Horn played were life and death. The arena was nature's arrant, cruel cathedral — the Arizona Territory: five hundred thousand square miles bordered on the north by the Colorado River, curving west to the California frontier, east toward the Dragoons and south along the Rio Grande and the Mexican border.

But the marauding Apaches were no respecters of borders. Again and again they crossed into Mexico to escape pursuing troopers and to wreak havoc on the Mexicans, whom they despised and disdained. And there, ensconced in their phantom-like *rancherías,* the Apaches waited and mated until the time came to move to the north again and strike at the uncountable whites who had claimed and "civilized" the once proud Apache empire.

An Apache chief could accord a warrior no higher accolade than to grant him the title of Eagle as part of his name. Of all living things, the Apache held the golden eagle in the greatest respect and reverence. The golden eagle embodied those attributes which the Apaches considered supreme: courage, vigilance, swiftness, and independence.

When an Apache chief perceived all these elements commingled in a brave, that brave was granted the honor of attaching the title of Eagle to a descriptive word as part of his name: Soaring Eagle, Searching Eagle, Racing Eagle, Warring Eagle, and Dancing Eagle.

When Cochise, one of the bravest, wisest, most respected Chiricahua chiefs, made peace with Al Sieber after many fierce encounters, he took the chief of scouts as his blood brother. During that ceremony Cochise bestowed the highest possible honor on his former adversary.

From that time on, Al Sieber's Indian name would be the Eagle — no other descriptive word. The purest, the highest, — the Eagle.

And now the Eagle had sought out Horn again. Once again each man knew the stakes would be life and death.

The wickiup was a rude framework of saplings covered with hides and brush. It had one entrance, facing east. There was a small fire in the center of a little scooped-out place. Horn and Sieber sat and ate while Suwan fed the hungry baby from her milk-filled breast.

The Indian woman could not have been more than twenty. She was copper-colored, with fawnlike eyes set wide apart and with long lashes and narrow eyebrows for an Apache.

"You weren't easy to find," Sieber said.

"How long you been looking, Al?"

"Ten sleeps. You winter here?"

"Yep."

"That your papoose?"

"Was a cold winter."

"Uh huh."

If Suwan understood she gave no indication of it.

"What you doing this side of the Rincon, Al?"

"General Crook sent me to fetch you. He's getting up an expedition."

"What for?"

"For Goklaya."

"Again?" Horn chewed on a tender piece of fowl. "Crook'll just chase that old panther to the border, then have to turn back."

"Not this time." Sieber wiped at his mouth with the worn edge of his sleeve. "The general's worked out a deal with the Meskins, some kind of 'hot-trail treaty.' He's going in. Wants Tom Horn to go with him. Two-hundred-dollar bonus, one hundred twenty-five a month."

"Starting when?"

"Starting now."

Horn looked at Sieber. "Let's start."

Both men rose. Sieber looked at Suwan. The baby had fallen asleep against Suwan's exposed breasts. She gazed at the child with the slightest trace of a smile on her generous red lips.

"Good-looking squaw," said Sieber.

"Yep." Horn nodded without glancing at Suwan. "Maybe I'll winter with her again next year."

A rope-thin old Indian walked out of the second, smaller wickiup but paid Horn and Sieber no attention as the scouts mounted up.

14

"What about your other horses and possibles?" Sieber asked.

"Ought to leave ol' Pedro and his grand-daughter something . . . besides that papoose."

"I reckon," Sieber agreed. They started to ride. "We got to make one more stop."

"Calculated we would." Horn pulled down on the brim of his hat and patted the mane of Pilgrim, his sure-footed buckskin.

The two men rode all day and into the night, as they had done many times. They rode in silence, with only their horses' hoofbeats serenading the soft, wind-chased sand.

To many, especially strangers, Sieber seemed a somber man, a man of few words and dark and murky moods. But the white and red scouts who served under him respected him — and feared him. Sieber never ordered his scouts to do anything he hadn't done and wouldn't do again. He was a man of justice — but sometimes justice had to be cruel.

Horn had witnessed many acts of kindness and compassion on Sieber's part, acts Sieber did his best to camouflage. He was a man of perplexing paradoxes — quiet, inert, passive one moment, a lightning bolt of fury the next. One time Horn watched

15

as Sieber twice quietly warned a renegade Apache to cease brewing the forbidden *tizwin*. The third time the Indian went for a weapon, Sieber decapitated the hapless red man with one swift stroke of a Bowie knife.

Sieber was not one to speak of his beginnings, but bit by bit, through countless campfires and whiskey bottles, Horn had pieced together the tapestry of his mentor's life.

Sieber was born along the upper Rhine in Germany on the leap year day of February 29, 1844, one of seven children with a father soon dead. His mother and brood emigrated to the United States and settled in Lancaster, Pennsylvania, near Conestoga Creek, then moved to Minneapolis, Minnesota, in 1856. As a boy, Al hunted and trapped. During the Civil War when barely eighteen, he enlisted in the First Minnesota Volunteers, a well-blooded outfit. He fought at the Battle of Fair Oaks, at Antietam and Fredericksburg, and the following spring at Chancellorsville. By then young Sieber was the crack marksman in his regiment. He served with valor at the second Battle of Bull Run and at Gettysburg, where he was wounded in the head and the leg.

Sergeant Sieber convalesced at York, Pennsylvania, and mustered out of the Yankee army with several scars and three hundred dollars. In 1866, civilian Sieber headed west to San Francisco and went to work on the Central Pacific. Later he herded horses from California to Prescott, Arizona, where he came under the tutelage of an army scout named Dan O'Leary.

From that time on, Al Sieber's experience and reputation as a scout, hunter, and marksman swelled to legendary proportions.

Now, once again, Tom Horn was riding with that legend — Al Sieber, the Eagle.

An hour after sundown the two men reined in their weary animals. Through the damp darkness Horn could barely make out the sign at the crossroad: "VALVERDE 5 miles, West" and "COLD-IRON 10 miles, East."

"Valverde, five miles," read Horn.

"Then Rosa's henhouse is just down the road a piece," said Sieber.

Within ten minutes Horn and Sieber arrived at the isolated two-story wooden building. They dismounted, tied off their animals, and walked onto the porch. There were lights inside. Horn tried the door, then knocked. No answer. He knocked again. Finally a coarse female voice answered.

"We're closed up."

Horn banged on the door harder.

"Go away. We're closed up!" The voice responded louder. Horn looked at Sieber, shrugged, then kicked the door in. Both men barged through the shattered door into the parlor and surveyed the surroundings.

Several señoritas of assorted hues, sizes, and states of undress were present. There was a bar, fashioned of planks nailed on barrels. A heavy stairway led to a second floor and a half dozen closed doors.

Rosa approached the two intruders. She was a big woman who had seen better days and nights. One of her eyes was missing, and its lid had puckered shut a long time ago.

"If you're the law," Rosa said, puffing on the soggy butt of a cigar, "check with Sheriff Pickens. He's already been paid."

"We're not the law," said Horn.

"Who are you?" Rosa's dark tongue reached over her upper lip and licked at an errant splotch of cigar leaf trapped in the stringy strands of her moustache.

"We're hunters," Horn replied.

"Well, go hunt someplace else," Rosa barked. "We're full up."

"We're looking for a man," said Sieber.

"You'll find a man, all right," Rosa cackled.

From behind Horn and Sieber a huge mastodon of a creature — a lascar or Oriental — close to seven feet tall made a grab for both men.

Horn moved faster than Sieber, who was caught in the giant's grip. Horn slugged the giant across his overhung jaw with all the might he could muster and with no visible effect. Horn picked up a chair and with pantherine grace broke it over the mastodon's head. The mastodon just grunted.

The señoritas laughed. Rosa cackled. Sieber, still in the giant's hawser hold, banged his fist into the mastodon's ribs.

Horn drew his .44 and smashed the barrel as hard as he could across the behemoth's shaven skull. The giant swayed slightly as a curious look came over his pocked face. Horn brought the gun barrel down hard on the peeled skull again, this time rupturing the boney surface and causing blood to spew. Still holding Sieber, the giant crashed like a gut-shot buffalo across a table filled with bottles and glasses, bringing Sieber down with him.

"Well, I'll be dipped in *tizwin*," said the naked, handsome, dark-skinned Indian who had appeared at the railing. "If it ain't Al Sieber and Tom Horn."

The best-looking whore at Rosa's emerged naked from a room and stood next to the young Indian, who had hold of a Colt Peacemaker pointed at Horn.

"Yeah, it's us, Kid," said Horn. "You can lower your weapon."

The Apache Kid flashed a quick grin, revealing twin rows of even, salt-white teeth. He was in his mid-twenties. He had blazing black eyes, and wore his hair shorter than the Apache but longer than the white man.

The Kid's grin grew wider. "What's a couple of nice fellows like you doing in a place like this?" he laughed.

Two hours later, Tom Horn, Al Sieber, and the Apache Kid lay naked in three large copper tubs. The men were being lathered and rinsed by three smiling señoritas whose wet gossamer garments outlined every upland and valley of their damp, dark skin. Each of the men smoked a cigar and drank from his individual whiskey bottle. In truth, the three weren't completely naked. Around his neck each wore a thong to which was attached an eagle claw.

The three scouts had worn them for almost seven years.

After a campaign against the great Mimbreño chief Vittoro, Sieber, Horn, and the Apache Kid had escaped into the furnace-hot desert. Sieber had been wounded, and the three scouts were afoot, half-starved, parched, and without canteens.

The Kid had spotted a golden eagle high on a crag. With the single shot he had left, Horn brought down the bird. They drank its blood and ate its stringy meat. Then Horn and the Kid carried Sieber to Fort Whipple. Sieber gave them each a claw of the eagle. It was an adoption procedure stronger than any proclamation by a court of law. From then on they were his sons.

"Sibi's Boys," was what the white man called them. In Apache, they were "the Claws of the Eagle."

"What're you two cloud hunters up to?" The Kid winked at his señorita and looked at Horn and Sieber.

"I been nursing my rheumatism at Bowie," said Sieber, "and Tom went back to the blanket for the winter."

"How long you been hibernating here, Kid?" asked Horn between puffs.

"I lost count," the Kid smiled, and looked at his señorita again.

"What do you use for money?" Horn inquired.

"Sometime back I took three hundred dollars from a couple of dumb white-eyes in a poker game. Thought maybe you two was them. They were so dumb they wouldn't trade a deuce for three aces."

"Cold deck?" Horn asked.

"Their deck," the Kid smiled, "but after a while it warmed up to me."

"Kid" — Sieber's eyes squeezed into more serious slits — "me and Tom are gonna wear off the winter fat scouting for General Crook again. Thought you'd want to sign on."

"Scout for ol' Gray Wolf? Why would I want to do that, when I'm rolling in . . ." — the Kid's eyes rolled around at the scrubbing señoritas — "money?"

"How much of that three hundred you got left?" Horn asked, running his hands through his soap-soaked hair.

"Don't know." The Kid shrugged and looked toward Rosa, who was igniting a fresh cigar. "Rosa, what's my tab?"

Rosa always carried a tally book. She

flipped it open and referred to the Kid's account.

"Including them" — she pointed to Sieber and Horn — "and the damages . . . two hundred eighty-seven dollars and fifty cents."

"Well," shrugged Horn, "you can't roll very far on twelve dollars and fifty cents."

"Guess I'm signing on," the Kid laughed, and reached both hands toward his señorita's ample breast. "*After* I spend that twelve dollars and fifty cents!"

Chapter 2

General George Crook tapped an Apache arrow against the map of the Arizona Territory and Mexico that hung on the wall of his spartanly furnished headquarters office at Fort Bowie.

"Last week Goklaya and his broncos hit the Olang ranch . . . here. Burned it down — wiped out the whole family, took over a hundred horses, and pulled for the border."

Crook waved the arrow back toward Horn, Sieber, and the Apache Kid. These four men understood and respected each other. The scouts knew that Crook was the best "wilderness general" who ever lived. He wore civilian clothes except for a well-seasoned, well-wrinkled old army jacket. Crook stood more than six feet tall, erect, spare, sinewy, and muscular. His voice was raspy, and he was severe and brusque in speech but not unkind.

With exception of the Civil War, he had spent his entire army career fighting Indians. Still, no American general was more respected, admired, and even loved by the red man. Crook made damn few promises, but kept the ones he made.

Born in Ohio, he graduated from West Point in 1852 and was assigned to California and the Oregon Territory. He subdued the Humboldts, then the Rogue Rivers and the Shastas, who had been marauding the mining camps. Crook was successful in campaigns against the Klamaths and the Tolowas and then the Columbia River tribes.

During the four-year bloodbath of the Rebellion, Crook distinguished himself at South Mountain, Antietam, Chickamauga, and Appomattox. Then it was back to Indian campaigns. Against the Paiutes he took to the field with a command of forty men wearing his old clothes and carrying a toothbrush. He didn't see a house again for two years. The Paiutes were made peaceable.

Later Crook led the great Apache campaigns that culminated in the surrender of five thousand of the boldest, bloodiest warriors on the face of the earth. They capitulated to Gray Wolf on April 6, 1873, at Camp Verde and became reservation Indians.

When Custer and the Seventh Cavalry were massacred by the Sioux at Little Big

Horn, General Crook was ordered north to the Platte. With only a hundred more men than Custer had had, Crook crushed the Sioux, the Cheyennes, and the Arapahoes.

But hundreds of Apache broncos had bolted the reservations, and Apacheria was a battleground again. Crook had been ordered back to Arizona, along with Sieber, Horn, and the Kid the Fourth and Fifth Cavalry hunted, trapped, or killed every warring Apache chief except for Goklaya.

And now General Crook had sent for Sibi and his sons . . . the Eagle and his Claws.

"Al, you, Horn, and the Kid've crossed the border illegally, chasing renegades." Crook cleared his throat in mock seriousness and added, "Without the army's knowledge, of course. Well, this time it's going to be legal — and the United States Army's going in with you."

"Not as much fun, Gray Wolf," the Kid grinned.

"Goklaya's *ranchería* is in the Sierra Madre, somewhere around here." Crook tapped the arrow against the map again, this time below the Mexican border. "We're going to find out exactly where and wipe it out."

Horn waved his hand at the map. "General, I've never heard of one country letting a foreign army cross its borders."

Crook walked back and forth in front of the map as he talked. "The Mexican government wants to get rid of Goklaya as bad as we do — maybe worse. So they're making an exception. Goklaya doesn't know that. He won't be expecting us. That's in our favor."

"That's about *all* that's in our favor," said Horn.

"Rugged country," commented the Kid.

"Million places to hide," added Sieber.

"Yes. Well, Goklaya's only in *one* place." Crook pointed the arrow at each of the scouts. "And you three are going to take us to it. What do you say to that?"

"I say," Horn remarked, "we better get started or we'll be late for breakfast in hell."

A few minutes later, Horn, Sieber, and the Kid were heading across the compound of Fort Bowie. Bowie was on the northeastern slope of the Chiricahua Mountains at Apache Pass. It stood at an elevation of more than forty-seven hundred feet on a slanting espadrille of the mountainside and commanded a fifty-mile view. The fort was peopled by civilians, Indians, and miners as well as soldiers. In addition to the barracks, there were a way station, a cantina, a sutler's store, a freight office, barns, and about a dozen other buildings. Fort Bowie had no walls.

"Ol' Gray Wolf sure is determined." Horn lifted the brim of his hat with his thumb.

"So's Goklaya," the Kid said.

"Yeah," Horn nodded. "Should be some party."

"*Skookum*," the Kid beamed.

Sieber handed Horn a folded sheet of paper. "Tom, here's a list of the supplies we'll need from the store. Me and the Kid'll check out the animals. Meet us over at Van Zeider's livery."

"You bet." Horn took the paper and went on his way.

Tom Horn walked into Ryan's General Store, looked around, saw no one, then hollered out.

"Hey, Ryan, you cabin-robbing bastard, where are you?"

A handsome, fair-haired woman in her mid-twenties stepped through the curtains from the back room.

"That cabin-robbing bastard is dead," she said.

"Dead?" Horn almost whispered the word.

28

A tall, sharp-featured, well-dressed man about forty followed the woman from the back room as she spoke again.

"Murdered," she added.

"Mr. Horn's been away from Fort Bowie for some time." The tall man's voice dripped caramel. "Evidently he hadn't heard of the tragedy."

"Horn?" the girl brightened. "Are you Tom Horn?"

"Yes, ma'am."

"I'm Shana Ryan, Tim's sister. He wrote of you often — said you were a friend. I'm sorry if I . . ."

"How'd it happen?"

"One night last month a thief broke into the store." Shana Ryan took a step closer to Horn. "Tim caught him at it but was killed."

The tall man glanced at his gold pocketwatch. His outward calm was betrayed by a pair of restless, narrow, ocherous eyes.

"Probably some crazy Indian," he conjectured.

"Or some not-so-crazy white man," said Horn.

"Oh, yes, I forgot," the tall man smiled. "Mr. Horn has an affinity for our red brothers . . . and *sisters*."

"Van Zeider, I don't like you." Horn

29

looked directly at the tall man. "I wouldn't like you any better if you were red, yellow, black or blue." He turned toward Shana Ryan. "I'm sorry about your brother, Miss Ryan. Are you still in business?"

"Well, Karl has made me an offer . . . for the franchise . . ."

"I'll bet he has," Horn said without looking at Karl Van Zeider.

"But in the meantime," Shana continued, "I'm still in business."

Van Zeider patted at the gold watch now in his vest pocket.

"Excuse me, Miss Ryan. Please consider my offer. It's fair. I might even say it's generous." Van Zeider smiled his confident, satisfied smile, nodded again at Shana Ryan, and walked stiffly past Horn and through the door.

When Van Zeider was gone Shana smiled at Horn. Even when she smiled there was a hint of sadness in her wide, opaline eyes. Horn guessed the sadness was for her murdered brother. She was the handsomest woman he had ever seen at Bowie and most other places. Her flaxen hair was pliant, but not too soft. Her body was athletic, but unmistakably woman. Shana must have weighed twenty pounds more than Suwan but it was disbursed in all the right places.

"It seems," she said, "that you and Karl have different points of view about Indians."

"And other things." Horn nodded.

"But you're a scout. You fight the Indians."

"Yes, ma'am. The ones that have to be fought. That's my job right now. I'm trying to work my way out of that job. But not Van Zeider."

"What do you mean?"

"There are some who don't want the Indians too quiet."

"But why?"

"As long as the Apaches are stirred up, there's contracts to be got. The War Department allocates over two million dollars a year inside the Arizona border. Those contracts mean big profits to some men. They supply the army with beef, horses, and mules. Then there's beans and bacon at forty and fifty cents a pound and flour at twenty dollars a hundredweight. And it all has to be freighted in. Van Zeider's in the freighting business — among other things."

"I never thought of it that way."

"Van Zeider does."

"Mr. Horn . . ."

"Tom."

31

"Tom, I just want you to know. . . ." Her voice drifted down.

"Yes, ma'am?"

"Well, as I said, my brother thought of you as a good friend."

"We were that," Tom Horn said and handed the supply list to Shana Ryan.

At the corral near the Van Zeider Bros. Livery and Freighting stable, the Apache Kid was examining mules as Sieber sat on a keg of nails and watched. Also watching was Emile Van Zeider, Karl's younger but huskier brother. He was a big bronco of a man, with a mouth that could hold a pint. Emile and three of his teamsters stood glowering at the Kid's judgment of their animals. General Crook was a great admirer and advocate of the mule, making extensive use of it during his campaigns and in time of peace. Crook always rode a mule, never a horse. He made certain his animals were selected with the greatest care. With specially designed harnesses and adroit loading procedures, Crook's pack mules could carry 350 pounds apiece, almost double the usual army mule load and nearly as much as the British army's elephants in India. The Apache Kid was the best judge of horse and mule in the territory.

The Kid looked at Sieber and nodded yes for an animal, then two no's in a row.

"There's nothing wrong with that animal," Emile Van Zeider barked.

"There wasn't ten years ago," the Kid grinned.

"Well" — Van Zeider pointed — "the other one's in good shape."

"One good lung and three good legs."

Van Zeider moved toward Al Sieber.

"Sieber, you're too damned particular."

"Look here, Mr. Van Zeider," Sieber said, spitting out some tobacco juice, "you get a dollar twenty-five a day for each of these mules. That's more pay than a trooper gets. You're damn right we're particular."

As the Kid rejected another animal, Pete Curtain, one of the big teamsters, stepped toward the Indian.

"Let's look this redbelly over — see what shape *he's* in." The teamster grabbed the Kid and promptly got caught with a left hook that knocked the big man into the dust.

The other two teamsters jumped at the Kid as fists flew. Sieber watched unconcerned while the two men flayed at the elusive, weaving Apache Kid.

Tom Horn appeared from around a

corner. "Hello, Al."

"Hello, Tom. Put in that order?"

"Yep. You didn't mention that Tim Ryan was killed."

"I guess I didn't."

The altercation continued, with the two teamsters beginning to get the better of the Kid.

"Got the mules picked yet?" Horn inquired.

"Not quite," said Sieber.

"Hold him, Pete! Bite him limp!" Emile Van Zeider hollered. "Give it to him, Jud!"

"Seems to be an honest difference of opinion," Horn said, observing the one-sided fight.

"That redbelly attacked my men," Van Zeider growled at Horn.

"All three of 'em?" Horn said. "Al, seems like the odds are always against the Indian."

"Seems like." Sieber spat again.

Horn tugged down the brim of his hat and moved toward the melee — not fast, not slow. Emile Van Zeider made the mistake of grabbing Horn. Horn flung a fist forward in a tight lump against Van Zeider's face, breaking his nose and knocking him galley west through the rail.

Horn picked up a heavy bucket and

rapped it hard against a teamster's head, sending him sprawling into a mule, who kicked and hee-hawed. A couple of other mules also made themselves heard and felt.

Emile Van Zeider started to get up, but Sieber's boot came to rest heavily on his chest. The Kid's fist smashed the remaining teamster senseless against the wall of the barn, just as General Crook appeared with Karl Van Zeider.

"Mr. Sieber," Crook announced in almost theatrical formality, "I'd like to hear your explanation of this."

"Yes, sir." Sieber spat once more. "Couple of jackasses started a fight."

Chapter 3

The dawn broke warm and gentle across the crowded compound at Fort Bowie. Crook's command waited as the general mounted his powerful gray mule, Apache.

The command consisted of forty troopers, a caravan of mules loaded with supplies and ammunition and twenty Apache scouts. Horn, Sieber, and the Apache Kid were mounted next to Crook as Captain Bourke, Crook's aide-de-camp, who had a lot of army between his belt, rode up.

"Captain Bourke," Crook said, "let's move out."

Bourke gave the command and the column moved, past the Van Zeider brothers, who were standing in front of the Van Zeider *cantina,* and Shana Ryan's general store. She stood watching shading her eyes from the glint of the morning sun.

As Horn rode by, Shana lowered her hand in a way that Horn interpreted as a farewell salutation. He nodded in return.

They headed south through the sun-burnished Arizona Territory, Crook at the head astride Apache with a shotgun across his saddle. Behind him rode the crusty, craggy officers, the nail-hard troopers, the leather-tough Indian allies — and the scouts, the lifeline to the others. With their finely-tuned senses and honed instincts, the scouts were a peculiar breed — part man, part wildcat — who could *feel* the hazards ahead.

And those "hazards" were Apaches.

"Apache" — the word came from the Zuni tongue and meant "enemy." And the Apaches were the enemy to anyone who tried to take their land, as they themselves had taken it in an unremembered time.

The Apache spoke a dialect of the Athapascan tongue and later Spanish. From the Mogollan Rim southward across the dreaded desert waste to the sky-piercing peaks of the Sierra Madre in Mexico — all this the Apache conquered. They scattered the Zunis out of the heartland, chased the Comanches to the east and the Yumas to the west, and carved their claim in blood and fear.

For more than two hundred years the Apache tribes had ruled the hard, cruel land. The Apache nation was made up of many tribes: Tonto, Mimbreño, Mescalero,

Jicarilla, White Mountain, Lipan, Pinal, Arivarpo, Coyatero and Chiricahua. The last and most cunning chief of the Chiricahua, Goklaya, still raided and killed, then melted like a phantom into the nearly impregnable mountain ranges of Mexico.

Goklaya had no more than a hundred Apache warriors, but they could make forty-five miles a day on foot, seventy-five on horseback, and when his horse fell the Apache would eat it and steal another.

Often the Apache preferred to move and fight on foot. Over much of the terrain in which the Apache excelled in guerrilla warfare, a horse was a handicap rather than an asset. The Apache was swift and noiseless and better off without some stupid animal who might snort or whinny at an inappropriate time — or leave tracks. The Apache warrior needed less food and water than the cumbersome mount he rode. He was a smaller, more maneuverable target on foot, with catlike speed and silence. But when he did use the animal in fighting or fleeing, the Apache was nearly as good a horseman as his Comanche cousin, whose cavalry puissance was peerless.

Whether afoot or mounted, in alkali dry

desert or on rain-drenched promontory, the Apache, man for man and pound for pound, measured up as the most defiant and dreaded enemy ever encountered by the United States Army.

It had been estimated that it cost the United States government five thousand dollars to kill an Apache. There was no way of measuring the price in human life and pain in defeating the facile Red foe.

These were the last of Crook's enemies — and Sieber's, Horn's, and the Apache Kid's. The rest of the Apaches had been "pacified" on reservations, in accordance with Crook's policy, a policy opposed by other United States Army leaders, who favored a different policy — extermination. . . .

At dusk, a scout who had been sent ahead signaled from a rise. Horn, Crook, Sieber, the Kid, and Bourke rode toward the vantage point. As the group arrived, the scout pointed toward a dust cloud moving far below. Bourke broke out his field glasses.

"Indians?" Crook asked.

"No," said the Kid.

"He's right, sir," Bourke confirmed, looking through his field glasses. "Not Indians."

"Soldiers," said the Kid.

"Right again," Bourke corroborated.

"Hibernating in that henhouse didn't hurt the Kid's eyes none," commented Sieber.

"Can you make them out?" Crook asked Bourke.

"Stars," said the Kid.

"What?" Horn inquired.

"Stars." The Kid touched his shoulders with both hands.

"A general?" Crook asked.

"Four stars." The Kid held up his right hand, thumb against the palm.

"There's no such thing as a four-star general," Crook said, with a trace of impatience.

"*Two* generals," the Kid grinned.

"It's General Sheridan, sir." Bourke lowered his field glasses.

"Who's with him?" Crook asked.

"Don't recognize him, sir," Bourke replied.

"Whoever he is," the Kid added, "he's done up in a heap of fuss and feathers and more brass than a ten-dollar spittoon."

The two contingents converged at sunset. General Philip Sheridan, General Nelson Appleton Miles, and their troopers reined up as Crook and his men approached.

Sheridan and Miles presented studies in startling contrast. Phil Sheridan was a small man, with the largest part of his head forward of his ears. He was a combative man, restless of spirit, not politic in language. His black-Irish bloodline was evident in his long, mobile face. He had the reputation of being sharp and peppery, a self-reliant man of courage and decision, a tactician. Sheridan was also a friend of Crook's.

Nelson Appleton Miles was a much bigger man, with a trace of weakness in his girth. He had a pleasant enough face above a fat neck. His plump hands seemed effete. His skin was thin and resented the outdoor rigors. Miles's reputation was that of a "headquarters general." He wore an overdone uniform of his own design. Next to Miles rode Captain Crane, a sunny-faced, intelligent young officer.

Crook waved at Sheridan. "Phil, you're a little wide of your mark, aren't you?"

"George," Sheridan responded, "you know General Miles."

Crook nodded. "You've not come after Goklaya too, have you, Phil?"

"No, there's bigger fish to fry," said

41

Sheridan. "And speaking of fish, which we're not likely to get out here, how about some supper?"

A million stars pierced the blue-black sky as the men ate and drank coffee around the campfire. General Crook rubbed at his side with his hide-hard hand.

"That Apache arrowhead still troubling you?" Sheridan asked.

"Mostly after I eat. That's something else I owe Goklaya."

"Well, George," said Sheridan, lighting a cigar, "you're not going to pay him back."

"Meaning what?" Crook frowned.

"It means I'm ordering you up to the Platte again."

"When?"

"Tomorrow morning."

"But Goklaya —" Crook started to protest.

"Goklaya is one bad Indian," Sheridan interrupted, "with less than a hundred followers. The Dakotas are swarming with six thousand Cheyenne and Sioux."

"The Cheyenne and the Sioux are at peace."

"They were when you left." Sheridan watched the smoke of his cigar as it blended and vanished into the dark sky.

"But they're painted again. And doing something called a ghost dance . . . following a 'messiah' they call Wovoka."

"I know Wovoka," Crook said quietly.

"And you know Sitting Bull," Sheridan said, "and Big Foot, Kicking Bear, and all the rest of the Oglala and Hunkpapa chiefs. That's why you're going north. General Miles is taking over your command."

"He's going after Goklaya?" Crook did not look at Miles, who sat stiffly nearby.

Miles answered for Sheridan. "Not personally. Captain Crane will lead the expedition. I'm going on to Fort Bowie."

Crook looked hard at his friend General Philip Sheridan. "Phil, with all due respect to the captain, he's going to be up against —"

"Oh, come on now, General," Miles interrupted. "I believe that the myth of the red man's superiority over the white race has been greatly exaggerated. I don't believe the red man is superior physically and certainly not mentally; that his fiber, sinew, and nerve power is of a finer quality; that his lungs are of greater development and capacity to endure the exertion of climbing these mountains than those of our own men like Captain Crane."

"Maybe," said Crook, "but General,

there's only been two animals to scale and survive on those Mexican ridges — the mountain sheep and the Apache. Phil" — Crook tossed a pebble into the campfire — "after all this time can't you wait —"

"I can wait, George." Sheridan spoke with the calm authority of the seasoned soldier he was. "But I'm not at all sure about those six thousand painted Indians. Are you?"

It was a question that didn't need answering. Crook flung out the dregs of his coffee and walked toward his scouts, who had heard the conversation. As Horn and the Kid watched, Sieber produced his canteen and poured some fluid into Crook's cup.

"I've learned one thing after twenty years of being in the United Stares Army," said Crook. "It's pointless to *argue* with the United States Army."

"Army's right, this time, General," said Horn.

"You brought in Custer's killer," Sieber added. "Made peace in the Black Hills."

"Gray Wolf's big medicine up there," the Kid added.

There was a moment of silence, broken only by the crackling sound of the campfire and a coyote wailing in the desert, waiting for an answer that never came. Then Horn spoke softly.

"We'll get your panther for you, General."

"Watch out that panther doesn't claw our young captain." Crook motioned his cup toward Crane.

"He'll learn," said Horn.

"Some learn." Sieber poured drinks into the scouts' cups. "Some die."

"They'll die if they listen to that over-stuffed book soldier," Horn added.

"General Miles has waged a lot of successful campaigns," Crook said.

"Not against Apaches," Sieber snorted.

"Can't buy Apaches like he bought his commission," Horn grinned. "His best strategy was when he married General Sherman's niece."

"She's a fine lady," Crook responded, "and I want you men to promise to help him. That's my final order. Will you do that?"

The three scouts nodded.

"I've got a feeling," said Crook, "that this is our last drink together. I want to thank you men. . . . I . . ."

"Enough said, General." Sieber raised his cup. "It's a creation-big country, but trails cross. We'll have another drink together somewhere, sometime."

Crook lifted the cup to his lips. "In heaven or hell," he said.

"I hope it's someplace in between." Horn smiled, and the four friends drank.

Chapter 4

April is the crown jewel of the desert. In April, the desert glitters with variegated plants, flowers, and aspiring life. Bright, shimmering cholla cactus, golden crocus, pink verbania, and flaming-red ocotillio blooms; quail, rabbit, and wild turkey scamper among their squads of young. April is the time of rebirth, with spring rain bathing newborn birds and chasing the winds of winter while washing the ferns and fondling grass. April is a time of seedling hope, of budding promise when things begin to bloom and move across the desert. And early that April morning the soldiers, scouts, and animals moved and then diverged: Crook, Bourke, and Sheridan to the north; Miles to the northeast; Horn, Crane, and their expedition to the south, toward the border and Goklaya.

With every mile the terrain became more rugged and wild. Captain Crane rode next to Horn.

"Beautiful country," said Crane.

"It is, but don't trust it."

"I don't see any signs of Indians."

"Yeah, well, when you see Apache signs be careful. When you don't see 'em, be *more* careful."

"Mr. Horn, I had a little talk with General Crook last night. He has the highest regard for you and Mr. Sieber and . . ." Crane pointed toward the Kid.

"He's called the Apache Kid."

"Mr. Horn, about these Indians . . ."

"What about them?"

"They fight their own people. . . ."

"Crook's strategy," said Horn. "Use Apaches to chase Apaches."

"I presume he got the idea from the British — use colonials to fight colonials."

"I presume." Horn nodded.

"Why do they choose to fight on our side?"

"Maybe they want peace." Horn shrugged. "Or maybe they want pay."

Horn was in no mood for trail talk. He could have further educated the young captain on the subject but chose to break off the conversation. Horn's eyes, mind, and senses stayed with the task ahead, with the hunt and the killing that would come if they found Goklaya — or if Goklaya found them. In this kind of warfare, the element of surprise was infinitely more important than manpower or firepower. Usually whoever hit first won.

Call it surprise, sneak, or ambush — that first unexpected attack meant victory. And it was up to the scouts to provide that element. Crook used few white scouts against the Apaches; most of his scouting contingent were Apaches.

Why *did* Apache fight Apache? Pay? Peace? Yes, and more. Long before the white man sought out and settled Arizona, there was deadly rivalry among the tribes even as there had been among the ancient Greek city-states. One tribe raided another, not just for territory and certainly not for crops — these people were hunters, not farmers. There was an unending need for one tribe to prove its superiority over another — a restless, irresistible drive to swoop and raid, steal horses and women, and claim victory over a worthy enemy.

Now, for years, the older chiefs and warriors, pent up and moribund on torpid reservations, had been boasting and taunting the younger bucks with tales of past glory.

It was no wonder that when Crook gave these young natural hunters and warriors an opportunity to leave the placid confines of the reservation and reap a new glory, they leaped at the chance. He hired rival tribes to chase the renegades and payed them well in money and in what the Apaches loved most of all — adventure. Besides, in this way the young Apache bucks could claim revenge for bloody raids the renegades had often made on the defenseless reservations.

Horn and Crane rode in silence until a question occurred to the captain. "Mr. Horn, in an encounter, how can we tell our Indians apart from the hostiles?"

"You'll notice," Horn pointed, "all our Indians wear a scarlet headband."

"The Apache Kid doesn't."

"He's different," Horn said in a hard voice. "There's another way of telling."

"How's that?"

"In an encounter, Captain, the hostiles'll be trying to kill you. There's the border."

Late that afternoon the lowering sun threw long shadows from the sawtooth peaks of the Sierra Madres. Beige sand stretched toward the blue-black rock that tore into the hot, clinging sky. The expedition was miles into Mexico, past the no-hurry *río* into wind-whipped canyons, moving toward the mountains that belonged to God and the eagles.

One of Sieber's Indian scouts rode up

fast. Sieber, Horn, and the Kid reined in. So did Crane, as the Indian's winded horse snorted and plopped to a standstill. The scout spoke in Apache.

"What is it?" Crane asked.

"Apaches," said Sieber. "Hit a ranch about two miles west."

"Well, let's go," Crane responded eagerly.

"Save your animal, Captain," said Horn. "It's too late to do those people any good."

It was.

When Horn and the others arrived, the burned-out ranch was still smoldering. The contingent dismounted and found at least eight bodies, so horribly mutilated that Captain Crane vomited.

The Apache Kid approached, carrying an empty whiskey bottle.

"American?" Sieber asked, pointing to the label.

The Kid nodded and handed the bottle to Sieber. Horn surveyed the devastation. "Took the cattle and the women. May as well bury what's left of the rest."

The Kid motioned toward the retching young officer. "Something he ate?"

Crane wiped his palm across his mouth and breathed heavily. "I . . . I've seen men killed before, but never anything as savage as this."

"Dead is dead." Sieber spat.

"Bad for them," said the Kid, pointing toward the hacked-up bodies, "but good for us."

"What does he mean?" Crane asked Horn.

"He means — now we've got tracks to follow."

Chapter 5

The column moved deeper into Mexico.
Sieber rode ahead. The Apache Kid was nowhere in sight. Neither were the other Indian
scouts. Crane kept his horse paced next to
Horn's buckskin. Suddenly, in the heat of
the desert, Captain Crane's body shuddered
as if he were suffering a severe chill.

"What's wrong, Captain?" Horn asked.

"I can't get the sight of those mutilated
bodies out of my mind."

"Apaches don't like Mexicans."

"They have a grisly way of showing it."

"Yep," said Horn. "Every chance they
get. Always been that way."

"Why?"

"*Quién sabe?* Maybe because a long time
ago the Apaches started raiding the villages, so the Mexicans started offering re-
wards for Apache scalps."

"Money?"

"Pesos. A hundred pesos for a male
Apache scalp, fifty for a woman's, twenty-
five for a child's — male or female. No
questions asked."

"Is this still going on?"

"Yep. Bad blood, and old Goklaya's got a couple of reasons in particular."

"What reasons?"

"Some years back the Rurales raided a Chiricahua camp and massacred some warriors and women, including Goklaya's mother and his brand-new bride — girl named Alope."

"Mr. Horn, you seem to know all about Indians."

"Nobody knows *all* about Indians." Horn pointed toward Al Sieber. "Sieber comes closest."

"I don't think your chief of scouts likes me."

"Why say that?"

"He hasn't said three words to me in three days."

"He's got nothing to say."

They rode for another hour before Crane spoke again. "I thought you said we had tracks to follow."

Horn nodded.

"I don't see any tracks, Mr. Horn."

"The outriders do."

"What do you mean?"

"I mean you can't follow Apaches' tracks directly, Captain. If you do they're liable to double back and 'bush you. Got to do it panther style."

"Panther style?"

"Yeah. We're going parallel to 'em. Cross once a day, then travel parallel on the other side."

"That's why we've been zigzagging?"

"That's why. They've already split up. Main bunch took the cattle. There's five of them kept the women. Probably played for 'em."

"What do you mean, 'played'?"

"Gambled," said Horn. "Apaches like a game called monte. And even if they don't like Mexicans, they'll mate the women and produce sons who'll kill more Mexicans."

Just then the Apache Kid galloped out of a ravine toward them. He pulled his horse up to Sieber, as Horn and Crane also approached.

"They'll never be in a better spot for us," the Kid beamed.

"John Six-Killer!" Sieber hollered. "He Dog! Hump!"

Three Apache scouts joined up with Sieber. Sieber waved and rode off. The Indian scouts followed. So did the Apache Kid.

"Captain," Horn said to Crane, "you stay here with the troopers till you hear gunfire. Then ride toward it."

Horn galloped away.

"But . . ." Crane looked around and exclaimed to no one in particular, "What the hell is going on!"

Chapter 6

At the makeshift camp there were five nearly naked Apache broncos and three completely naked Mexican captive women.

Two of the women were heavy and across their broad backs and thick legs were bloody lines where the Indians had taken switches to their bodies to urge them along on the trek. The youngest girl was thin and wide-eyed, with long, straight black hair that fell to her small, upturned breasts. She was unmarked except for those breasts, which had been pinched and twisted and cruelly abused by one of the Apaches as she rode in front of him astride his horse.

The Indians laughed, drank, and played monte. In the pot were rosaries, clothes, and other effects of the stripped and frightened women, who hunkered nearby, ignored for the moment.

Horn, Sieber, the Kid, and the other scouts silently crawled into vantage spots around the camp.

At a signal from Sieber, he and the scouts opened a deadly crossfire with their

Winchesters. Two Apaches dropped instantly, dead. The third managed about four steps, then stopped with a neat hole between his eyes and the back of his head blown away. The fourth made it a little farther — just a little, but with the same result.

The fifth and final Apache ran like a burning cat toward an opening between two boulders. As he passed through he was greeted rudely by the stock of Horn's rifle, swung by the barrel. The rifle butt smashed the Apache's flat face even flatter.

"You killed them!" Captain Crane cried out when he arrived and surveyed the carnage. "Butchered them all."

"All but one, Captain," said Sieber. "He's gonna take us to Goklaya."

"Better see to the women, Captain," Horn added. "This ain't gonna be pretty."

It wasn't.

The surviving Apache, his face battered, was tied upside-down to a tree. Already several razor cuts had been sliced across his belly and breast. Blood seeped down his chest, across the cartilage that had been his nose, into his eyes, and off his long black hair onto the ground.

The Apache Kid had done the carving as Sieber and Horn watched. Sieber spat and nodded again. The Kid's knife blade gently stroked across the Apache's chest again, producing another fine red line.

"Reluctant, ain't he?" Horn said to Sieber as Captain Crane strode over.

"Mr. Sieber," Crane fumed, "I can't allow this. . . ."

Sieber paid no attention.

"No, you can't, Captain," Horn said evenly. "So why don't you take a walk? Won't be long now."

"It won't be long before this man bleeds to death."

"You want to find Goklaya?" Horn asked.

"Of course I do," the young officer replied. "But . . ."

"There's no worse death for an Apache," Horn said, "than to be strung upside-down and bleed to death."

The Apache Kid picked up a handful of blood-soaked dirt and let it filter through his fingers.

"His spirit's doomed to wander down below, Captain," said the Kid, "instead of up there in the heavenly hunting grounds."

"He'll tell," Horn added.

Sieber nodded, and the Kid started to

slice again. At the touch of the blade the Apache screamed a ghostly scream that echoed through the dark canyons. The Kid smiled and relaxed.

"You see, Captain," Horn said pleasantly.

Later, Tom Horn gave the Mexican women food and talked to them in Spanish. They were shrouded in army blankets and clung to their rosaries. Captain Crane stood nearby.

"Gracias, señor," said the oldest woman.

"Por nada, señora," Horn replied, then walked away as Crane followed.

"Poor, miserable creatures," Crane intoned. "What kind of a life will they go back to?"

"Better than the one they had ahead of them," Horn answered.

"Yes," Crane admitted.

As they walked past the Kid, who was eating some pinole bread, he looked up at them.

"Hey, Tom," the Kid smiled, "that young Nellie ain't bad-looking . . . in the dark."

Horn and Crane kept moving toward Sieber. Al sat across the sliced-up Apache, now secured by strips of wang.

"Mr. Sieber," Crane inquired, "when

will we get to . . . the enemy camp?"

"Tomorrow night," said Sieber; then he rose and walked away. Crane watched after him for a moment, turning to Tom Horn.

"Mr. Horn, I wouldn't say you waste words, but that man won't spare an extra syllable."

"Rheumatism," Horn remarked.

"Well," Crane admitted, "he does know his business."

"No better man ever followed a set of tracks," said Horn, "without leaving any."

Chapter 7

The next evening just after twilight surrendered to darkness, the troopers silently surrounded Goklaya's *ranchería*. The unsuspecting village was anything but silent. Lulled by the seeming security of an international border and isolated within a spectral sanctuary high in the hidden peaks, the warriors, along with their squaws, sweethearts, and children, were celebrating the spring feast of fertility — Fermaga.

The mountain meadow flickered with dozens of fires and echoed with sounds of jocularity. Music, chanting, dancing. Dogs barked and livestock bellowed and brayed. *Tizwin* and whiskey overflowed into the mouths of drunken warriors. The Apache braves' powers of fertility would be tested far into the night, but now they drank and, from the fires, ate venison, goat, and dog.

Goklaya had posted no sentries.

Captain Crane had the good sense to deploy his force as Sieber suggested. When the time came, half the command would charge on horseback; the other half on foot and from all directions. A dozen of the best riders would run off Goklaya's horses, then join the attack.

Horn inhaled the odor of mesquite smoke and smiled.

"We can thank the feast of Fermaga. They'll be at it most of the night."

"You think Goklaya's down there?" Crane asked eagerly.

"He's there, all right." Horn nodded and pointed to the largest wickiup.

"Ol' Gray Wolf'd give both his stars to be here now," the Kid said.

"Then now's the time to hit 'em," Crane volunteered.

"No," said Sieber.

"We hit them tonight," Horn added, "Goklaya'll melt into the dark."

"Well, what *do* we do?" Crane inquired.

"May as well get some sleep," Horn said. "Dawn's the time. They'll be dead to the world."

"In more ways than one," the Kid grinned.

Sieber slept. So did the Apache Kid. Tom Horn lay awake. His eyes followed the descent of a falling star as it disappeared into the blue-black sea of sky.

Within hours the last of the Apache renegade bands would also fall. There would be blood on grass and rock and stream. The blood of the renegade Indians and of troopers and scouts. That was inevitable. Destined. Would it be Horn's destiny to die and be buried in some unmarked grave in an unnamed place?

Tom Horn thought of his dog Shedrik, buried long ago on the Missouri farm of Horn's youth. Tom's father still plowed that farm. The elder Horn was of Pennsylvania Dutch stock as hard as the earth he turned for the spring planting. But Tom Horn, unlike his half dozen brothers and sisters, wasn't meant to be a farmer, to milk cows and spread seed and marry some brood woman who also would bring forth seven sons and daughters.

Tom hated the hoe his father handed him before his eighth birthday. Even then he yearned for a rifle. He'd often skipped school and followed tracks of rabbit, skunk, coyote, and on rare occasions even a wildcat. When he was twelve Tom got himself a rifle and skipped school even more often. With his dog Shed, he'd follow tracks and bring home game. His strong, stern father usually rewarded him with a whipping while his mother watched silently and without sympathy.

And often Tom would silently watch the

caravan of prairie schooners creaking west through Missouri clay stretching toward the flat prairies, across the muddy Red River, through the vast Llano Estacado, west into the wind-slashed canyons over the Mescalero Ridge, always west — toward their manifest destiny. Tom Horn knew that it would be *his* destiny, and soon. Meanwhile, he reveled in the stories of Missouri's living bad men. Frank and Jesse James were still riding and robbing and with them the Daltons and the Youngers, unreformed guerrillas from Quantrill's Raiders who had splattered Missouri and Kansas red with blood. But the outlaw life never appealed to Tom. He had never stolen so much as a tomato and never would. Tom Horn would earn what he got — not from farming, not out of the land, but off it, hunting.

When he was fifteen, after scores of whippings, mostly for forgotten reasons, the climax came. A neighbor boy thought it great sport to shoot down dogs. He emptied both barrels of a shotgun into Shed. Tom caught up to his dog's killer and thrashed him senseless. With tear-flooded eyes, young Tom Horn buried Shed, then went home, only to receive another whipping because his clothes were torn.

The older man struck his son with a leather harness. This time Tom struck back. But Tom was no match for the bigger, stronger man, who beat him with hammer fists and left him a bloody heap with broken face and ribs.

A week later, when he could walk, Tom Horn took up his rifle, kissed his impassive mother, said goodbye at Shed's grave, and sought his own manifest destiny — west.

While he couldn't whip his father, Tom was big and strong for his age. He worked his way west on the railroad as a section hand to Dodge City — the Dodge City of Wyatt Earp and Bat Masterson. Tom landed a job in a livery stable. He loved horses and would ride every chance he got. Then he got a chance to be a cowboy. He signed on as a drover and helped take a herd to Santa Fe across the trail that John Simpson Chisum had blazed a few years before. In Santa Fe he rode shotgun for Overland Stage and then moved farther west to Arizona. In Prescott he secured a job delivering beef to the Indian agency.

At Fort Whipple Tom Horn met the man who should have been his father and became just that — Al Sieber, chief of scouts. Al took an immediate liking to the tall, handsome lad who had a natural proclivity for riding, shooting, and hunting. Both men spoke German and Tom managed to pick up a lot of Spanish. He had a quick facility for language.

With Sieber was a young Indian not quite Tom's age. Tom heard that the young Apache's true name was Ski-Be-Han, son of an obscure chief called Togo-De-Chug. Years ago, the chief's few followers had deserted him and held him up to ridicule, considering him inept, ineffectual and a drunken sot. Even his squaw left Togo-De-Chug and their infant boy and went to live with another brave. The boy suffered the derision and laughter directed at his father until the night the broken chief died drunk in a pigpen.

Sieber felt sorry for the orphaned lad and took him in. The youngster rarely left Sieber's side. Sieber was everything the old chief hadn't been. He was strong and respected. No one laughed at Al Sieber, chief of scouts. The lad wished that Al Sieber was his father. The young Apache learned to speak and think and even feel as a white boy would. Sieber called him Kid, and as he grew his true name was almost forgotten and he became known only as the Apache Kid.

Tom Horn lay near the now quiet meadow where Goklaya and his followers slept. For some it would be their last before the final sleep. Horn thought of the years since that meeting at Fort Whipple . . . Sieber, the Apache Kid, and Tom Horn — the Eagle and his claws. . . .

Sieber taught Tom Horn how to think like an Indian. At the same time he taught the Apache Kid how to live like a white man. He enlisted them both as scouts more than a decade ago.

Together they rode for Crook against the great Apache chiefs Mangas Colorados, Vittoro, Eskiminzin, Loco, Chato, Cochise. All those chiefs were dead now — all but Goklaya.

And through the years Sieber taught Horn and the Kid what he called the great commandment from nature's bible: "Every living thing wants to go on living."

Every living thing wants to go on living — the Indians in the village below, the troopers and scouts who were now awake and at the ready, the Apache Kid, Al Sieber, and Tom Horn. Yes, Tom Horn wanted to go on living. He reflexively checked his Winchester and his .44. How many lives that wanted to go on living had these weapons taken? Tom never kept track. How long would it be before someone took his life? Tom rarely thought of that prospect — but he thought of it now.

He also thought of a young woman he had seen but twice and spoken to only once. Not just a brood woman, Shana Ryan was made for more than having children. She was obviously well educated, a capable woman, strong yet feminine. There was something in those eyes that bespoke deep emotion, even passion. Those strange male stirrings swelled in Horn, and he wished he could put his arms around that ripe, well-turned body and feel the warm tenderness of those soft red lips.

Maybe when he got back to Bowie . . . if he got back . . .

The campfires below were cold white ashes. The warm April dawn spread softly across the moist meadow. From one of the distant wickiups a baby cried but not for long. A mother's breast provided milk and promised safety and there was silence again.

The braves below outnumbered the troopers and scouts almost two to one.

Then there were the women and children, some of them capable of making war.

There could be no compromise, no negotiation, no bloodless surrender. If the situation were reversed the Apaches would not hesitate. They would attack and hit hip and high without warning, as they often had on white and Mexican villages and even on their own people.

Horn looked toward Sieber. The Apache Kid glanced from Horn to Sieber. Captain Crane's eyes, already grown older, were fastened on the chief of scouts.

The Eagle gave the signal to attack.

Chapter 8

Horn, astride Pilgrim, followed at hoof and heels by the Apache Kid, led the attack and headed straight for Goklaya's wickiup. Horn and the Kid kept up an alternating barrage of lead aimed at the wickiup's entrance. Whoever was in there would have to stay in.

The village erupted with screams, human and animal, as from every point of the compass death lanced out of the barrels of rifles and guns. The attack was devastating and, from a military point of view, an almost immediate success, turning the quiet village into an abattoir.

The yelling cavalry charged at Goklaya's remuda and succeeded in scattering the frightened horses. Several of the wickiups were set afire and the flames and smoke added to the chaos. Dogs barked, babies cried, and squaws screamed because death was not for the braves only. Women and children caught in the crossfire fell upon the already fallen, lifeless bodies of their husbands and fathers.

Charging horses lurched, twisted, and slipped in the soft, moist earth as troopers flew off their mounts onto the retreating Apache braves.

Sieber yelled commands, and Captain Crane yelled them again and carried them out. His soldier's instinct and training prevailed, and Captain Crane never paused to consider the deaths of the innocents, because unless all resistance was crushed, he, too, might be dead at any moment.

Horn and the Kid, both with Winchesters in hand, leaped off their mounts and raced toward the entrance of the large wickiup.

Goklaya and two squaws were tearing off a back section of the structure as Horn and the Kid smashed through the front entry with pointed rifles. Both squaws, gripping knives, plunged at the intruders. Without hesitation the Kid swung the stock of his Winchester, clubbing one squaw on the side of the skull, as Horn's rifle butt broke the other squaw's knife wrist, then plunged into her rib cage, knocking her to the floor.

Goklaya realized that it was too late to try to fit through the small, jagged rupture at the rear of the wickiup. He spun like a frenzied cat and with the same movement pulled a knife and a Colt .45 from his silver-studded weapons belt.

Just as Goklaya's gun cleared the black-leather holster, Horn fired his Winchester. The bullet shattered the barrel of the chief's Peacemaker, and blood splattered from the palm of Goklaya's right hand. But the Indian's left hand, still holding the hunting knife, raced at Horn's throat with the full weight and strength of Goklaya's body behind it. The Indian was too quick and too close for Horn to fire his long gun again. But Horn was too quick for Goklaya's knife, which missed its twisting target by a hairsbreadth.

Horn and Goklaya fell to the ground, grappling in a whirlwind of fury. The fingers of Horn's right hand clawed and dug into Goklaya's wrist as the gleaming blade of the Indian's knife quivered less than an inch from Horn's eye. The scout's left hand grabbed a mass of Goklaya's hair and tore the chief's head backward, giving the Apache Kid a clear and unmoving target. The Kid quickly whacked his Winchester's barrel across Goklaya's forehead, knocking him off Horn and onto his back.

In the next instant the tip of the Apache Kid's long gun pressed against Goklaya's nose, and the great warrior knew he had been captured.

Outside in the village, most of Goklaya's

73

braves who were not already dead suffered the same fate. About a dozen had vanished into the rocks and narrow ridges. The body count, excluding women and children, was at least twice that number. Of the remaining warriors, nearly half had suffered wounds before throwing down their arms in surrender.

The wails and moans of the wounded and the crying of women and children still pierced the camp as Horn and the Kid stepped out of the wickiup's entrance, holding Goklaya between them. Then, as if an unseen blanket smothered the village, there was silence.

All living eyes, Indians' and troopers', froze on the great Apache chief. There was blood on his hand and head.

Then Sieber motioned to Crane, and the two men moved forward. They stopped a couple of feet from the brace of scouts still holding Goklaya.

"Captain Crane, meet your prisoner Goklaya," said Horn. "Around here the Mexicans call him Geronimo."

At last Horn had said the word *Geronimo*. Sieber, the Kid, Crook, and Horn had vowed never to speak that name until the last of the warring Apache chiefs had been subdued. The other officers and men knew and respected that vow. They, too, had sworn never to call him by his bloodstained name until he was dead or captured.

Now the deed was done. The word could be spoken. Geronimo stood captured, bloodied but unbent. By sight his age was indeterminate. He might not have been fifty, but actually he was more than sixty. He was tall, nearly six feet, and broad of chest. He had a terrifying countenance, with black, bullet-hole eyes that reflected cunning and hate but never fear — even now. He had a hawk nose and a thin slash of mouth that, because of an old wound, drooped to the right in a perpetual sneer.

Geronimo had been captive before, but never before by force. Always he had surrendered voluntarily, when it suited him — when the snows painted the peaks above the timberline and winter drew close and cold. When there was no grass to graze his herds, no food to feed his followers and no ammunition to kill his enemies, Geronimo would call for a *yoshte* with the white man's army. He would agree to go back to San Carlos and be a reservation Indian. A good Indian.

And then in the spring, with full bellies, Geronimo and his followers would bolt the reservation on stolen horses, with guns and ammunition enough to start a new war until he wanted to surrender again.

But this time he hadn't wanted to surrender. Geronimo had been beaten by those more cunning and crafty and as cruel as he. There were the dead women and children as testament to that cruelty. Geronimo had not only been captured, but he had been humiliated. He stared at the Apache Kid, then spoke.

"*Hayasaha-more.*"

"What did he say?" Captain Crane asked.

"Nothing much," Horn answered. "He swears to kill the Kid."

Geronimo turned his face and spoke to Horn. "Nan-Tan-Lupan."

"Gray Wolf's busy," Horn replied. "He sent us little lambs instead."

"*Yoshte,* Nan-Tan-Lupan," Geronimo said.

"You can tell that to Captain Crane. And you'll have to tell him in American."

Geronimo looked at the young captain.

"I want to talk with my friend General Crook."

The young captain spoke with surprising authority. "You'll have to talk with General Nelson Appleton Miles."

Chapter 9

Fort Bowie turned out in full parade for the proceedings. At Sieber's suggestion, Captain Crane had sent a rider north across the border to dispatch word of Geronimo's capture.

But strangely there were no cheers at the sight of the returning troopers, scouts and their prisoners. The civilians, soldiers, miners, and other citizens of Fort Bowie stood without words at the wonder of the event. Geronimo and the remnants of the bloodiest brigade of renegades in the southwest — or anywhere — marched to the beat of hooves and drums. They were horseless and weary, many of them still streaked with the now brown-dry smears of their own blood.

As the procession moved past Ryan's store, Horn looked for Shana. She was there on the porch. She smiled, even more beautifully than Tom remembered. This time there was no mistaking the wave. Horn touched the brim of his hat and rode with the rest toward headquarters.

General Nelson Appleton Miles stood in

full and splendid regalia, shiny as a newly minted silver dollar. Somewhere he had liberated a long white feather of some sort, and apparently in the belief that it added a splash of dash, bravado, or gaiety, he had planted it at a jaunty angle on the brim of his cavalry hat. In truth, it looked ridiculous.

Captain Crane saluted and spoke to his commanding officer. "General Miles, your prisoner. Geronimo."

Besides raiding, killing, mating, smoking, and drinking, Geronimo was partial to talking. He considered himself an outstanding orator, the equal of Satanta, the Kiowa chief who was known as the Great Orator of the Plains. On the occasions of his past surrenders Geronimo had publicly speechified for the better part of an hour on the merits of his case. He saw no reason to make an exception in the present situation.

"You are the *nan-tan?*" Geronimo inquired of Miles, who looked haughty but blank.

"Leader," Sieber interpreted.

"I am," Miles confirmed with condescension.

"We make *yoshte,*" Geronimo proceeded. "Your soldiers — no, not soldiers; cowards to the core, butchers of squaws and babies — will pay with their unworthy lives. You bring me back to live on the reservation. I have been there before and tried to live in peace with seven other tribes who are our enemy. We are not farmers, but you make us plant crops. This we did among the sandstorms, centipedes, and rattlesnakes. But much of the land promised us has been taken away, bite by bite. Mormon farmers came and claimed the best land, poor as it was. Miners swarmed in from both sides and dug out metal they call copper. We are given beef that only buzzards would eat. Indian agents use our warriors and children to dig coal for their own profit.

"We are not allowed to drink our ancient brew, *tizwin,* or cut off the nose of an unfaithful wife.

"Your soldiers and scouts sneak on our land like wolves in the night and carry away our women, who are never seen again. Soldiers hide along the ridges and use our men and women for target practice, and we have nothing to shoot back with but rakes and hoes.

"To these and many other wrongs you bring us back, to live not as men and women, not even as pets, but as a herd of worthless creatures, penned without pride or honor, groveling on our own ground for enough to eat — we who are hunters, with no man our equal.

"But Nan-Tan, you cannot hold Goklaya. I am not a pet. I am not a plow beast. I am not even a man. I am the spirit of all my people who came before me, whose bones are buried in our land. I will not sell those bones cheap. And I will not squat like a toad in the desert to be squashed by the boots and hooves of your troopers.

"I will ride free to the ridges, the highlands, and the mountains with the spirits of my ancestors."

Geronimo looked from Sieber to Horn; then his mad gaze locked on the Apache Kid.

"But first I will kill these three." Geronimo turned again to Miles. "What do you say to that, Nan-Tan?"

"Slap him in leg irons," General Nelson Appleton Miles replied.

An hour later General Miles sat behind his desk, the desk that had been Crook's, smoking a cigar. The desk and the map on the wall were about the only things that remained as a reminder of the "Wilderness

General." The room, no longer spartanly furnished, had been redecorated with pictures of Miles and other prominent people including Grant, Sheridan, Sherman, and of course, Sherman's niece, Mrs. Miles. Assorted flags, swords and miscellaneous mementos cluttered the room.

Horn, Sieber, the Apache Kid, and Captain Crane sat uneasily watching the cigar smoke twist and curl toward a hanging lamp while they waited on the words of Geronimo's "conqueror."

"Captain Crane," Miles said slowly and with deliberation, "I want to commend you on the speed, accuracy, and efficiency with which you carried out my instructions."

Crane squirmed with obvious and honest embarrassment. "Beg pardon, sir, but as you read in my report, it was these three men who deserve —"

"Yes, I read your report, Captain." Miles blew out another patternless cloud of blue smoke. "You're too damn modest. You and the rest of my command did a first-class piece of work. And now with Geronimo's capture we can close the book on the Apaches."

"Yeah, well . . ." Horn stroked at his lean, stubbled chin. "Geronimo can open

81

that book up again. You heard what he said, and he broke out of San Carlos before."

"He won't escape this time," Miles smiled. "I'm sure of that."

"It's good to be sure," Sieber observed.

"He won't escape," Miles added, "because I've made arrangements to ship him and what's left of his band to Fort Marion."

"You don't mean that swamp down in Florida?" Sieber spat some tobacco on the floor.

Miles took notice, then replied, "That's exactly where I do mean."

"Apaches can't survive in that swamp country," said Horn.

"Seminoles do," Miles countered.

"They're a different breed," Horn tried to reason. "Apaches are desert and mountain people. They're susceptible to swamp fever and a dozen other diseases."

Miles knocked ashes off his cigar. "Nevertheless, they'll leave by rail as soon as I arrange a few final details."

"It just don't . . ." Sieber started to spit again but swallowed instead. "It just don't seem right, General."

"It does to me." Miles smiled with supreme satisfaction.

"You know" — Horn rose from his chair — "this was their real estate in the first place."

"That's ancient history now. This is a new day, with new ways. And you men will have to get used to those ways too."

"Such as?" asked Sieber.

"Such as, Mr. Sieber, you and your men can draw the pay General Crook promised, then consider your job terminated."

The Kid spoke for the first time. "Terminated — that does mean 'done,' don't it?"

"It do." Horn nodded.

The Kid rose. So did Sieber, followed by Crane.

"Who's gonna scout for you?" Sieber asked.

"Nobody. The scout is obsolete, like the bow and arrow." Miles smiled with satisfied finality. "That's it, gentlemen. Thank you and good day. Captain Crane, I'd like you to stay a moment."

As the three scouts reached the door, Sieber let fly a spray of brown spittle.

Chapter 10

The three scouts went by the quarter-master's office and picked up their pay. Then, as they crossed the compound of Fort Bowie, they stopped in front of the black-smith's, where a large crowd had gathered. Horn, Sieber, and the Apache Kid paused and viewed the result of what they had been paid to do.

Geronimo, surrounded by soldiers, stood in the middle of the smithy's shop, which had only three side walls and an open front.

The smith and his two apprentices worked quickly and efficiently. From the forge they took red-hot strips of iron wagon tires about an inch thick and fash-ioned them into rings with protruding lips, through which they punctured rivet holes. Each of the two rings was linked together by a heavy chain less than two feet long.

The glowing set of ankle irons was tossed sizzling into a large basin of water to cool off. A couple of soldiers led Geronimo close to the anvil. The black-smith clapped an iron on one of the chief's ankles and hammered the lips shut. His apprentice carried a red-hot rivet from the forge. The blacksmith hammered it shut. The procedure was repeated on the other ankle, and the war chief of the Chiricahuas stood shackled.

Geronimo could no longer run or ride. He could only walk and stumble with heavy, halting steps. But he could still hate. And his eyes flashed hate at the three scouts. That hate settled on the Apache Kid. Without words, with an unspoken promise, Geronimo silently repeated his vow to kill the Apache Kid. And the Kid understood. So did Sieber and Horn.

The three scouts turned and walked away.

In Ryan's store, Shana had just sold Mrs. Dockweiler needles and thread and was walking the overweight and overtalkative woman to the door, when she caught sight of Horn and his companions.

Mrs. Dockweiler kept spewing out enough words to choke a cow, but now Shana heard none of them.

Since the day Tom Horn walked into the store, Shana had found herself thinking of no one else — except, of course, her brother, whom she had loved.

Tim had been easy to love — bright,

strong, and with a bent for laughter. After their mother and father died, Tim had made sure that Shana wanted for nothing. He had sent her to Wellesley, where she never quite fit in. She was accepted by the other girls and was even very popular, but in her heart Shana knew she wasn't really a part of all that. It was all too confining, too conforming. She wanted to be free of the confinements, the conformities. She wanted to move west like her brother. And now she was here — but Tim was dead.

There had been a young man, handsome and rich, from a Boston banking family. He loved Shana — or said he did. He would have married her. For a time they were unofficially engaged. He wanted to make it official, but then Tim died and Shana came west.

Brent Bradford was tall, rich, well mannered, well dressed, and well educated with all the attributes a Wellesley girl seeks in choosing a husband. But somehow when all the attributes were put together in making Brent Bradford, something had gone wrong — at least for Shana.

If Bradford had had to make it on his own he might have been a better and stronger person. He was born with not only the proverbial silver spoon, but an entire place setting. Since he was her only child after three miscarriages, his mother smothered him with comfort and sop. She saw to it that his every moment was carefree and consequently he cared for nothing except for Shana, or so he said. Bradford graduated from Harvard in the upper third of his class. Had he ever opened a book, he would have been class valedictorian.

Besides his easygoing attitude, there was something in his physical makeup that Shana resisted. There was something too moist in the touch of his hand, too dry in the touch of his lips — the few times Shana allowed his lips to touch hers. He was the sort who was pleasant enough company in a room full of people or even at a dinner party of four. But when Shana and he were alone there was an uneasiness.

And now there was Tom Horn. He was not what could be considered well dressed and probably slept in his clothes as often as not. And he was not well educated in terms of books. Shana had yet to touch his hand or lips, but she was not uneasy at the prospect. As for anything more, she tried to prevent herself from thinking about it. She didn't always succeed.

Shana watched as Tom Horn walked across the compound. His movement was strong and graceful, with long, smooth strides, a slight forward bend to his out-sized shoulders sloping down muscular arms to large rawhide hands. His head tilted a touch to the right, and his chin was always thrust ahead, giving the impression that he was smelling as well as looking where he was going. He appeared relaxed yet always ready to spring. Shana kept looking at him and even failed to acknowledge Mrs. Dockweiler's garrulous goodbye.

"What do you think ol' Geronimo'll do when he finds out what Miles's got in store for him?" the Kid wondered aloud.

"What can he do," replied Sieber, "with that iron bracelet on his legs?"

"Yeah," Horn snorted. "Well, fellas, how does it feel to be obsolete?"

"Feels thirsty," said Sieber.

"We can do something about that," Horn philosophized.

The Apache Kid pulled some of his pay out of his pocket and waved it around.

"Got enough to buy out Rosa's for a week or two. I ain't slept in a bed since you two busted up that party."

"Let's hit the saloon," Horn pointed toward Van Zeider's *cantina*. "I could use some good whiskey."

"Or *any* whiskey," Sieber added.

As the three scouts headed toward the *cantina*, Captain Crane, who had emerged from Miles's headquarters, moved quickly to intercept them. There was a troubled look on the young officer's face.

"Tom! Mr. Sieber! Hold up a minute, will you?"

"What's the matter, Captain?" Horn smiled. "Did General Miles forget to tell us something?"

"I . . . I'm sorry about General Miles's attitude. . . ."

"He's a fool," said Sieber, "and that's not his only fault."

"Forget it, Captain," said Horn. "That's ancient history."

"In my report I made it quite plain that Geronimo's capture was entirely your doing and without the three of you I'd probably be either lost or dead — or both."

"Never mind that, Captain," Horn replied. "You'll do to cross the river with and we'll miss Miles like a toothache."

"Maybe he'll change his mind," Crane said.

"Yeah," Horn grinned, "and maybe there's a herd of wild elephants in Tucson."

"Captain." Sieber touched the sleeve of Crane's tunic.

"Yes, sir?"

For the first time there was a trace of warmth in the old scout's attitude toward the young officer. "I've found that feeling sorry for yourself is a poor medicine, so would you consider joining three obsolete scouts for a drink?"

"Mr. Sieber," Crane gulped, "I'd consider it an honor."

As the four men proceeded in step toward the *cantina,* they crossed in front of Ryan's store. Shana had taken up a broom and was sweeping the porch, which she had swept an hour earlier.

Tom Horn's eyes took her in the way a stallion takes in the sight of a fine young mare. He hoped she didn't realize what he was thinking as he watched her body move and her hands direct the long stem of the broom across the spotless porch. She was dangerous, and Tom knew it. Not because she had aroused Tom Horn's mating instinct. Many women, Indian and white, had done that. But for the first time another instinct had been stirred in him. He wanted to hold her, soothe and protect her, to make sure she was not alone, to say things he had never said before. Dangerous!

90

"Welcome back, Tom." Shana stopped sweeping, brushed back a soft strand of an errant gold curl from her smooth brow, and smiled.

"Thank you Miss Ryan," Tom said a little uncomfortably. "Oh, this is Al Sieber, the Apache Kid, and a friend of ours, Captain Crane."

Shana nodded acknowledgment. So did the men.

"Haven't sold out yet?" Horn asked.

"Not yet."

With a trace of impatience, Sieber glanced toward the *cantina*.

"I'm thinking of staying," she added.

"Interesting," said Horn, and walked away with the others.

Chapter 11

Customers at the Van Zeider *cantina* were sparse. Fewer than a dozen sat in bunches of three and four at tables, and two others leaned against the bar and chinned with Peg, the bartender. No one knew or cared what Peg's real name was; since he had long ago been fitted with a wooden rig that substituted for his missing right leg, everyone called him Peg. He didn't seem to mind — particularly if the caller was buying him a drink. Peg was tall, more than six feet, and in his mid-fifties, with uncombed hair and an untrimmed beard. He wore a soiled, collarless striped shirt. Wide dirty suspenders held up a pair of frayed pants.

The three scouts and Captain Crane walked through the open door. Horn motioned for them to sit at an empty table near the window, then walked to the bar.

"One bottle," ordered Horn, and slapped money on the counter.

"I hear you boys treed that Apache son of a bitch." Peg waddled a step, picked up a quart of whiskey, and set it next to the money.

"Four glasses," Horn said.

Peg wiped at his whiskey-soaked whiskers, ran a dirty palm across his crop of mottled hair, and reached under the bar. He brought up a glass, then another, then a third. He hesitated, bit his yellow teeth into his lower lip, and looked toward the Apache Kid.

"*Four* glasses," Horn repeated.

Peg set up another glass.

Horn picked up the bottle with his left hand, stabbed the four glasses with the fingers of the other hand, and proceeded to the table where Sieber, the Kid, and Crane sat waiting.

As Horn walked across the room none of the customers drank or spoke. All eyes were aimed point-blank at the Apache Kid.

Peg leaned across the bar, poured a drink for a customer who hadn't asked for one, and whispered a few words. The customer, known only as Baldy, a wizened old coot, hairless as a sausage, nodded, threw the drink down his throat, and scuttled out the door as fast as his weedy curled legs could convey him.

Horn paused a beat and pointedly looked around at all the silent, staring citizens. That look from Tom provided incentive enough for the locals to go back to drinking.

Horn loosed the four glasses onto the table, then set the bottle directly in front of the Apache Kid with the label straight at him.

The Kid looked from the label up to Tom. It was the same whiskey the Indians were drinking at the ranch they turned into a slaughterhouse in Mexico.

"That brand sure gets around," said the Kid.

"Boys," said Sieber, "we can chew the cud of deliberation some other time. We're here to do some by God drinking with our ol' hunting partner Captain . . . Say, Captain, you must have a first name — most everybody does."

"Of course I've got a first name."

"Well, say it, boy," Sieber barked. "Say it!"

"It's . . . Melvyn."

"Melvyn!" Sieber roared. "Melvyn! Sounds like a by God minister."

Horn shoved the bottle toward Crane. "Well, Melvyn, go ahead. Pour."

Captain Crane poured.

"Did you see that, boys?" Sieber bellowed. "Filled all four glasses to the lip. Never spilled a dollop!"

"A good, steady hand," said Horn, li[ft]
the glass nearest him. "A toast. Gen[e]
George Crook!"

"General George Crook!" all repeated.

They drank.

"Pour," said Horn.

Captain Melvyn Crane poured.

"To the U.S. Army scouts!" he said.

"We'll get to the scouts later," Sieber declared. "General William Tecumseh Sherman!"

"General William Tecumseh Sherman!"
the voices echoed.

They drank.

"Pour," said Horn.

Captain Melvyn Crane poured. This
time several dollops overflowed onto the
already whiskey-stained tabletop.

"General Ulysses Simpson Grant!" Horn
toasted.

"General Ulysses Simpson Grant!" the
words charged back.

They drank.

"Pour!" Horn and the Kid exclaimed simultaneously.

Emile Van Zeider, escorted by five of his
brawniest goons, entered and stood near
the doorway. Peg nodded toward the
Apache Kid. Van Zeider moved with heavy,
deliberate steps, and his goons fanned out
in a half circle rimming the window table.

"entlemen," said Van Zeider, "there's n some mistake."

"Not yet," said Horn.

"Go away," Sieber added, "before you make one."

"Me and my friends here aim to set something straight." Van Zeider moved a step closer.

"Yeah," said Horn. "Well, me and my friends've been near enough to hell to smell smoke. And we aim to do some snorting! So go away. There's a lot of generals we ain't drunk to yet. Pour."

Captain Crane poured.

"You and your friends can drink to every soldier in the United States and Russian armies, but" — Van Zeider pointed to the Apache Kid — "not *him*. Not in here."

"Why not?" Horn asked evenly.

"We don't sell whiskey to Indians."

"Don't you?" Horn said just as evenly.

"It's against the law."

"Is it?" Horn lifted his glass. "General Philip Henry Sheridan!"

"General Philip Henry Sheridan!" the others repeated.

They drank — all but Horn. Van Zeider's hand shoved against his elbow, causing the scout to spill some whiskey.

"Look what you did," Horn said calmly.

96

"We don't sell whiskey to Indians," Van Zeider repeated.

"That ain't no Indian," Sieber said calmly. "That's my son."

"Your son, my ass. He's a redbelly, and we don't sell whiskey to Indians."

"I heard you say that," Horn nodded. "I also saw some Indians who drank your whiskey, then butchered a Mexican family."

"You're a liar!" Van Zeider growled, and gripped a handful of Horn's shirt at the shoulder.

"Get your satisfaction, you son of a bitch!" Horn leaped to his feet and smashed the fisted knuckles of his left hand into Van Zeider's cheekbone.

The Kid had already selected his target and in an instant buried a swift, breath-busting fist into a goon's breastbone. Sieber broke the whiskey bottle across the brow of another victim, but Captain Melvyn Crane was the unfortunate recipient of a foul blow behind his ear. However, Sieber repaid the ungallant blow-giver with a kick to the shank. Crane recovered quickly and delivered a crunching punch into the dastard's teeth.

After that the brawl got better. Chairs flew, and so did fists, elbows, bottles, and boots. Some of the customers unwisely chose to join in on the side of the house. They mostly got in the way of the goons, who could've used more professional assistance.

Peg waddled up and down the bar, yelling unheeded advice to Van Zeider and company. Van Zeider took another blow from Horn that flung him over a table toward the bar. Horn turned his attention in the direction of the fracas. By now Sieber had assumed a lofty, less assailable position atop the unlit iron stove and was overseeing the proceedings with detached amusement.

The Kid and Crane were left to their own devices.

Emile Van Zeider rose to both knees, shook some of the fog from his throbbing head, and pointed under the bar to Peg. The bartender nodded, reached below, and hauled up a shotgun. One hand on the barrel, the other on the stock, Peg tossed the weapon to Van Zeider, who was now on his feet.

Stock butted against his hip, Van Zeider aimed the shotgun toward Tom Horn. Fast as a wasp, the Apache Kid unsheathed a knife and threw. The knife stuck to the hilt in Van Zeider's chest. The shotgun tiled astray and went off, blowing the *cantina* window into bits and pieces.

General Miles and a covey of troopers appeared at the door, and things became suddenly quiet. Ridiculous white plume or no, Miles was still the commander of Fort Bowie.

Emile Van Zeider lay near the bar on the dirty floor. His eyes, mostly white, rolled upward and toward the left. His blanched, bloodless face twisted in pain. There was blood on his chest and more coming.

"Get that man to a doctor!" Miles barked.

Four troopers immediately rushed to carry out the command.

"It was that Injun!" Peg pointed at the Apache Kid. "That goddamn Injun throwed the knife into Van Zeider."

"Arrest him," Miles ordered.

Two troopers peeled off and went for the Kid. One of the troopers lifted the Kid's Colt from his holster and the other pointed toward the doorway.

The Apache Kid looked at Sieber, who nodded. The Kid walked ahead of the soldiers past Tom Horn, whose life he had saved.

Their eyes locked for an instant; then the Kid headed for the door.

Miles turned toward Al Sieber, who was still perched atop the stove. "Well, Mr. Sieber, what've you got to say?"

"I don't suppose, General," answered Sieber, "that you'd care to join us in a drink?"

Chapter 12

Shackled, Geronimo stood inside his cell gripping the iron bars as he watched the two troopers unlock the cell directly across from his. He could almost reach out and touch the Apache Kid. Almost. But Geronimo didn't want to touch the Kid. He wanted to kill him.

The iron bars clanked shut. A trooper twisted a key; then both troopers marched back up the narrow hallway dividing the two facing rows of cages.

The Apache Kid turned and ran his fingers across the lock. He didn't try to avoid Geronimo's stare. The two Apaches on opposite sides of the same war were now on opposite sides of the same cellblock.

Doctor Jedadiah Barnes had seen and stitched worse wounds — much worse. He said as much to Karl Van Zeider, who paced in the waiting room as the doctor came out of his office carrying the knife the Apache Kid had planted in Emile's chest.

Doctor Barnes, a venerable veteran of

101

Civil War battlefield medicine and scores of Indian campaigns, was an informal sort of fellow, a rumpled, rounded man with splotches of broken blood vessels splattered across his ruddy face. A set of steel-rimmed glasses framed a pair of owlish gray eyes and strings of silver-gray hair twisted onto the front of his bison brow. A perpetual silver stubble poked through his face. His shirt had survived many winters and few washes. His shiny blue trousers and matching vest were embedded with smeared stains of coffee, liquor, and blood, partly camouflaged by a ramble of wrinkles. Jedadiah Barnes took his medicine wherever he found it. He had found enough in Arizona the last dozen years to keep six doctors steeped in blood and stitches. He saved more patients than he lost. Of course, some of his patients lost arms, legs, and parts of organs in the process, but the majority kept on living. So would Emile Van Zeider.

Doc Barnes stuck the Apache Kid's knife into one of the posts that helped hold up the waiting room.

"He'll be fit to walk in a week, go back to work in two. He can start drinking whiskey again most any time. Deep wound but clean. Your brother was lucky, Mr.

Van. Two inches lower woulda split his heart like a ripe tomato. Damn lucky."

"Yes." Van Zeider looked at the knife sticking in the post. "Well, the Apache Kid won't be so lucky."

General Nelson Appleton Miles had declined Al Sieber's invitation to have a drink. Instead, he had ordered Sieber, Horn, and Captain Crane to report to his office.

The two scouts and the young officer, still showing the effects of the brouhaha, stood listening as the commander of Fort Bowie meted out his judgment.

"Captain, in view of your exemplary record up to now, I am going to forgive your curious behavior in the *cantina*."

"Thank you, sir." Crane arched to attention.

"However," Miles went on, "I strongly suggest that in the future you choose your companions with a great deal more . . . discrimination."

"Yes, sir."

Miles paused and focused on the two scouts. "You men will be held responsible for damages. Fortunately, Mr. Van Zeider will survive.

"What about the Kid?" Horn asked.

For a moment Miles savored the power of his command. Fort Bowie was like a ship at sea and General Miles was the captain. His word was law. But unlike a ship in the middle of a boundless ocean, there were appeals. However, appeals took time. Anything Miles ordered would be done and then — and only then — possibly reviewed. General Miles rested both elbows on the arms of the chair where he sat and slowly and deliberately tapped the edges of his fingers and thumbs against each other.

"The Kid, as you so quaintly call him, is as murderous as those other savages he's locked up with." Miles ceased tapping his appendages and peered over the edges of his fingers, which now formed a tepee. "And he's going to be treated exactly the same."

"What does that mean?" Sieber questioned.

"It means" — Miles broke up the finger tepee — "the Apache Kid's going to be shipped with the rest of them to Fort Marion."

"You can't do that!" Horn exploded.

"Don't use that tone of voice with me, Mr. Horn," Miles shot back quickly, "or you'll find out just what I *can* do."

104

"But sir, I —" Captain Crane started to speak, but Miles cut in.

"And you, Captain Crane, will be jeopardizing your career if you say one more word in this matter."

"Take it easy, Captain," Horn said, trying to calm the waters. "Look here, General, Geronimo's sworn to kill him. The Kid chose to fight with us and against them."

"He should have chosen," Miles replied, "*not* to try and kill Mr. Van Zeider."

"He had no choice," said Sieber.

"*Mr.* Van Zeider was aiming to blow me apart with that ten-gauge," Horn added.

"That hasn't been determined," Miles answered. "Maybe he was trying to stop the fight by firing a warning shot."

"Yeah," Sieber grunted, "right through Tom's back. Besides, if the Kid had wanted to kill Van Zeider, that Dutchman'd be deader than a canned sardine."

"General," Horn tried to reason, "you put him on that train and he'll never get off alive. You know that."

"I'll ship him in a car with the women, children, and wounded," Miles responded. "I'll give him that much consideration."

"What happens when he gets off the train?" Horn pursued.

105

"That will be all!" Miles dismissed the discussion.

"No, that won't be all, you perfumed peacock! . . ." Horn moved forward, but Sieber grabbed him.

"Hold it, Tom. That ain't gonna do any good. Come on, let's get outta here."

"That is a smart suggestion," said Miles. "It would even be smarter if both of you left Fort Bowie. The change of scenery might improve your temperament."

"Thanks for the advice, General," said Sieber as he nudged Horn toward the door. "But we ain't ever been accused of being smart. Vital, once in a while, but never smart. And as for our temperament, so far it's been down right see-date."

From the time of her arrival at Fort Bowie, Shana Ryan had found Karl Van Zeider to be a gentleman, charming and helpful. When Tim was killed, Van Zeider took it upon himself to write Shana a consoling letter telling her of her brother's death. In that letter he offered to buy the operation, saying that he would keep the store open until she replied. If she decided to sell, he would send her the money immediately.

Shana replied that she was coming west

106

to visit her brother's grave and that she probably would sell but would make her decision after thinking things over.

Shana had no strong ties to the East. Besides, she wanted to get away from Brent Bradford's ever-yeasting ardor. He was convinced that no reasonably sane woman could continue to resist the spell of his obvious charms. At the Boston train station he pressed those dry lips onto hers and rubbed his chest against her breast with what he considered passion and promised to wait at the bank until she returned. As far as Bradford was concerned, they were all but betrothed.

He had been waiting now at the counting house for more than two months, while writing seventeen passionate letters and receiving three polite but noncommittal missives in return. In his last letter Bradford had written that he was ordering an engagement ring that he had specially designed himself . . .

Karl Van Zeider met Shana at the railroad station near Fort Bowie and escorted her to her brother's grave. She ordered a headstone and had it placed.

Van Zeider turned over the profits from the store, meager as they were, and increased his offer from two thousand dollars to twenty-five hundred. Shana was sorely tempted to sell. Still, she felt near her brother here, walking where Tim had walked, touching the things he had touched, and putting fresh spring flowers on his grave.

She even harbored the hope that somehow Tim's killer might be found and brought to justice. But what justice? Suppose the killer were hanged? What solace would that bring to her — or to Tim Ryan in his cold, narrow chamber six feet beneath the earth?

Once again she listened to Karl Van Zeider's courtly, caramel-coated voice as he stood across from her in the store. Perhaps it was the things Tom Horn said and implied, but lately Shana had begun to get a slightly different perspective of this tall, helpful, courtly gentleman with the restless eyes.

"Shana" — Van Zeider reached across and gently touched her forearm — "are you listening to what I'm saying?"

"Yes. Yes, Karl — of course I am." His fingers were longer and stronger, but in a way his touch reminded her of Brent Bradford's — moist and covetous, not warm and comforting. "What were you saying?"

"That you seemed to be on another

108

planet," Van Zeider smiled. "Or maybe in Massachusetts. Were you thinking about that young man you've been writing to, Mr. Bradford?"

"I guess in a way I was," Shana replied, and changed the subject. "Karl, I'm glad your brother's going to be well."

"What? Oh, yes, so am I. Look here, Shana, you're a young beautiful woman. But the strain's beginning to show. All this is just too much . . ."

"For a young beautiful woman?"

"Exactly."

"I'd better take a look in the mirror, Karl. I didn't realize I was deteriorating so rapidly. Before you know I'll be scaring the customers away." Shana was beginning to enjoy vexing the worldly entrepreneur. " 'Oh, don't go into Ryan's Store!' I can hear the mothers telling their little children. 'There's an old hag in there. Some say she's a witch from Salem, a bony old hag with sunken eyes and a wart on her nose. . . .' "

"Oh, stop it, Shana!" Van Zeider smiled a forced smile. "That's not what I meant, and you know it."

"I'm sorry. I shouldn't tease. Karl, you've been a big help and I appreciate all you've done."

"Look here, Shana — you know my brother and I have most of the franchises from Prescott to the border. Fort Whipple, Lowell, McDowell, Apache . . ."

"Yes, I know."

"And it's our line that freights the goods in."

"I know that, too."

"I'm prepared to raise the offer to three thousand dollars."

"That's more than the store's worth."

"Probably, but not to me. I have plans, Shana. I intend to be a power in this territory."

"You already are."

"Not the kind of power I have in mind. Arizona's the crossroads of the country. Whoever controls this territory is a man to be reckoned with from the Mississippi to California. Give me five years, and I'll be . . ."

"Governor?"

"I don't *want* to be a governor." This time Van Zeider's smile wasn't forced. "Or a general or even a president."

"You just want to *control* all those people?"

Van Zeider's smile grew to a grin. "Let's just say I want to make sure all those people in high places are friends of mine."

Van Zeider's voice assumed an intimate tone. "And Shana, I'd like you to be a friend of mine. More than a friend."

Good God, Shana Ryan thought to herself, is this one proposing too? Will I end up with suitors from one end of the country to the other? Suitors who don't suit me? Or is it part of a promissory ploy by an ambitious, worldly man playing a game to get something from a vulnerable, guileless woman? But this was no time to weigh and analyze Karl Van Zeider's intentions. And at the same time she caught a glimpse of Tom Horn and Al Sieber walking toward the guardhouse. Their step was neither jaunty nor light. There was a thundercloud look in both faces. Her thoughts were broken by the sound of Van Zeider's voice.

"Shana, if you do sell, you don't have to go back to Massachusetts. There can be a fine future for you here in Arizona. But not as a storekeeper trying to grub out a living among soldiers and savages."

Fortunately for Shana, Mrs. Dockweiler entered the store at that moment and promptly let loose a long-winded litany while waving several spools of thread and railing about being sold the wrong colors. They didn't at all match the other thread she had purchased six months earlier from the dearly departed Mr. Ryan, and Miss Ryan ought to learn how to run a store or find someone who did.

Karl Van Zeider shrugged and smiled his charming smile, whispering to Shana, "Besides the soldiers and savages, I forgot to mention the overweight, bellicose female customers who are spoiling for a fight. Please think it over."

Shana nodded and as Mrs. Dockweiler discharged her declamation without so much as a beat for breath, Van Zeider left.

At least, Shana thought to herself, Karl Van Zeider has a sense of humor.

Chapter 13

The long, narrow stone guardhouse was built along the western slope of Fort Bowie's compound. A few slim slits embedded with iron bars served as windows but didn't afford the residents much of a view. The barred, unglassed apertures did allow the sizzling summer wind and dust to make the structure insufferably hot in summer and the ragged, ice-edged wind and grit to make it shivering cold in winter.

If a prisoner had to pick a season of residence, autumn or spring were the times. But that was little consolation to the Apache Kid. Horn and Sieber had no trouble getting in to see him. The guards were old friends. The trouble came in telling the Kid of Miles's decision. Both men leaned hard against the bars confining the former scout. Horn and Sieber tried to appear casual, even optimistic, but as Geronimo stood in the nearby cell and stared across at his infernal enemies, the words came in short, harsh whispers from the two scouts.

No matter how soft their whispers, they

knew that Geronimo would hear — if he hadn't somehow got word of the Kid's fate already. Secrets were short and few around Bowie, especially where Geronimo was concerned.

"Miles says he's shipping you to Florida," Horn said in a low voice.

"On the same train as . . ." Sieber motioned his head almost imperceptibly toward Geronimo.

The Apache Kid was stunned. He tried not to show it. It showed.

"Thought it was better you heard it from us instead of strangers," Tom added.

Maybe it was. Still, for the Kid it didn't do much to lessen the impact.

"Yeah, thanks," the Kid said, avoiding the eyes of both men.

"Look, Kid," Horn hastened, "it'll be days, maybe weeks before Miles arranges for that train. A lot can happen. We're gonna send a telegraph to Crook —"

The Kid interrupted, "You think that the Cheyenne or the Sioux will deliver that telegraph to ol' Gray Wolf?"

"We'll get word to him," Horn went on, "and Al's gonna go see the governor."

"They'll set Miles straight." Sieber nodded. "Him and his goddamn chicken-feathered hat, which he ain't got

114

much brains under."

"You know," Horn said, "the governor's a good friend of Al's."

"Hell, yes," said Sieber. " 'Zuly' owes me a fistful of markers."

"Tom . . . Al . . ." The Kid's voice seemed to come from another world. "You ever been locked up?" He was only inches away from the two scouts, but the distance couldn't be measured.

"We'll get you out, Kid," said Horn. "You've done a lot for the army."

"But I'm an Indian." It wasn't a statement from the Kid but an indictment.

Horn nodded. "Yeah, you're an Indian."

"Not to them I ain't." The Kid motioned toward Geronimo and the other locked-up Apaches. "So what *does* that make me?"

There was a stifling moment of silence.

"I don't know, Kid," Horn answered. "I don't know. But we'll do everything we can. Come on, Al."

Al Sieber reached through the bars and touched the Apache Kid's shoulder.

"You take care of yourself . . . Sibi's Boy."

Horn and Sieber turned and walked toward daylight. The Apache Kid gripped the bars until the blood flushed out of his fingers.

115

The sneer on Geronimo's face was closer to a smile than it had ever been — a smile of triumph.

"Sibi's Boy!" The Apache Kid let loose of the bars and allowed the blood to flow back into his cold fingers. He walked to the wall and inhaled the upstart summer air that wandered loose and free outside the guardhouse.

"Sibi's Boy." The Apache Kid touched the eagle claw at his throat. For years it had been a sign that he belonged to something, to someone — that he mattered.

"Sibi's Boy" — with the skill, strength, and advantages of his Apache heritage, he could look at the forest and the mountains and on the ground and read every sign there.

"Sibi's Boy" — who could also walk with pride and accomplishment in the white man's world and work for a white man's pay.

"Sibi's Boy" — who now hung suspended between two worlds, unclaimed by either, denied by both: reviled by the Apache, rejected by the white man.

"Sibi's Boy" — convicted and condemned. Was he really Sibi's Boy? Had he ever been?

Chapter 14

Horn and Sieber paused in the cool afternoon shade thrown along the east side of one of the adobe structures. Each man rolled a cigarette. Horn fired up a match on the seat of his trousers and lit Sieber's smoke, then his own.

Neither man had spoken in the few minutes since they left the guardhouse. The image of the Apache Kid confined in such a scant space seemed as unnatural as that of a panther in a purse. But a panther could tear his way out of a purse; the Kid was penned by stone and iron in a cell not much broader than the smile that used to be on his face.

"You know," said Horn, "maybe we're going about this from the wrong direction."

"Well, if you know another direction, point us toward it."

With thumb and forefinger Horn took the cigarette from between his lips and jabbed toward Dr. Jedadiah Barnes's office-hospital.

"What's the matter?" Sieber inquired. "You sick?"

"No, but an acquaintance of ours is. You remember our old friend Emile Van Zeider. Maybe we ought to pay him a visit."

"And finish him off?"

"No," Horn replied. "And eat a little crow."

Both men pinched out their cigarettes and started to walk.

"I'd sooner eat a centipede," Sieber said.

As Dr. Jedadiah Barnes walked into the room, Tom Horn pulled the Apache Kid's knife from the post where the crusty doctor had stuck it.

"From what I hear the Kid won't have much need of that thing where he's going, unless they let him hunt crocodiles," the doctor observed. "Al, how's the rheumatism?"

"I'll be cured just like the rest of your patients — when I'm dead."

"With all that lead in you, you should have been dead a long time ago."

"I been sent for, but I ain't went."

"Well, I got somewhere to go," Barnes said, snapping shut his worn and scarred medical bag, "so spell out what you came for. It's not like you fellas to waste time with giggle talk. Nurse Hatchet!" he hollered toward what served as the hospital ward. "Let's get a move on!"

Immediately a tall, razor-thin, middle-aged woman in a nurse's uniform appeared and took up a sliver of space in the doorway. She did in fact have a face like a hatchet blade, slender and severe. The effect was continued upward by the wide parting of her thinning hair directly in the middle of her head.

"Damn you, Jedadiah! I've told you a million times not to call me hatchet. My name's Thatcher, and after nineteen years at your elbow you damn well know it. *Thatcher!*"

"I did say Thatcher, goddammit! You must be losing your hearing along with your memory. Maybe I ought to get you an ear trumpet."

"You do and I'll know where to stick it! Hello, Al, Tom."

Both men nodded and smiled. They had been listening to the verbal crossfire between Dr. Barnes and his nurse for a long time.

"We've got to go and clean up what's left of those Apaches you boys shot up, if they don't die from the filth of that pigpen they been laid in," Doctor Barnes said, picking up his medical bag. "We got empty beds

119

here, but the army's afraid those redskins'll contaminate the white man's hospital. You never did say why you come by."

"We never got the chance," Sieber allowed.

"Well, you got it now. Speak up!"

"We're here to visit your patient," Horn explained. "Mr. Van Zeider."

A look of incredulity crept across Doctor Barnes's well-creased face. "You're the last ones I ever thought'd come to call on him. He's right in there, mean as a peed-on rattler — unless Florence Nightingale here just poisoned him. Matter of fact, his brother's in there with him. You get two for the price of one, and that's no bargain. Step right in: it happens to be visiting hours — always is."

Horn and Sieber nodded and started walking toward the ward.

"Just a minute," Doctor Barnes said, pointing to the Apache Kid's knife still in Horn's hand. "I wouldn't advise taking that thing in there with you. Might stir up some unpleasant memories. Well, come on, Nurse Hatchet; let's get a move on. The sight of you might shock some of them savages into recovery."

"If the smell of you don't kill 'em first," Nurse Thatcher declaimed as they

120

walked out the door.

There were eight beds in the ward. Emile Van Zeider, the only patient, lay propped on a bed near a window overlooking the compound. On a table next to him was a half-empty bottle of whiskey, and beside the table stood Karl Van Zeider, his usual serene self, smiling and twisting his fob on the gold chain laced through his vest.

"Well, this is a peculiar turn of events," Karl Van Zeider commented as Horn and Sieber entered. "Emile, look who's come to call on you."

Emile grunted and reached for the whiskey bottle.

"I know you're here to see Emile," Karl continued. "I couldn't help overhearing your conversation with the eccentric Doctor Barnes."

"Actually," Horn said, "what we've got to say concerns both of you."

"That sounds logical," Karl Van Zeider said, nodding agreeably, "since my brother and I are partners — not equal partners, of course, but partners nevertheless. Are you looking for work?"

"No, that's not why we're here," Horn managed. "We're here to ask you to do something — or I guess not to do something."

"I can't imagine what you would want — or not want — us to do. Can you, Emile?"

"No." Emile poured another double shot into the water glass in his hand.

"It's about the Apache Kid," Horn said.

"Oh, yes. I understand he's due to take a trip shortly, along with your other red brothers, to a more tropical climate."

"Van Zeider, I'm not here to argue the merits of Miles's decision where the rest of those Indians are concerned," said Horn. "That's another matter. But you know the Apache Kid's not like the rest of 'em."

"You hear that, Emile? Mr. Horn says the Apache Kid is not the same as the others." Van Zeider turned back toward Horn. "And why isn't he, Mr. Horn? Because he calls himself Sibi's Boy, shares lodgings and women with you two, and parades around the territory as if he were the equal of a white man? Is that what makes him different in your eyes?"

Both Horn and Sieber restrained the impulse to leap upon Van Zeider and tear the tongue out of his head.

"No, that's not what makes him different," said Horn.

"Then what does?"

"He's different because he chose to be different. And he's worked damn hard at it.

He gave up the ways of his people. He learned to read and write — and when the time came to fight, he fought with us and against them."

"For pay," Van Zeider smiled.

"Everybody works for pay, Van Zeider. You, your brother, Sieber, me — everybody. But everybody doesn't risk his life. The Kid did, again and again. If he'd ever been captured by any one of those tribes, do you know what they would've done to him? I don't think you and that civilized mind of yours could ever imagine. There's not a man, woman, or child in this fort, in most of this territory, that doesn't owe the Apache Kid more than any amount of money can buy. You don't measure the risks he took in money."

"What is the point of all this oratory, Mr. Horn? What are you soliciting?"

"I'm asking you and your brother not to bring charges. I'm asking you to go and talk to General Miles on the Kid's behalf. He won't listen to us — Crook would have — but what you say to Miles would carry an awful lot of weight. It might tip the scales for the Kid. If Miles turns him loose, we give you our word the Kid'll leave this part of the territory. You won't ever see him again."

"You forget one fact, Mr. Horn — among other facts — this passionate patriot of yours, this exemplary citizen, tried to murder my brother."

"And you forget that your brother here was about to squeeze off a load of shot into my back."

"That's a lie!" Emile barked. "Besides, I gave you all fair warning to get out!"

"That brings up another matter," Karl Van Zeider persisted. "For years while your precious General Crook was the high hickalorum around here, you people ran roughshod over everything and everybody. The rules weren't meant for you and your pampered scouts. You thought your boots were filled with something special."

"Come on, Tom," said Sieber. "Let's get out of here."

Karl Van Zeider went on, "You were breaking one of those rules in the *cantina* because no matter what you say or think, the Apache Kid is an Indian. But I'll say one thing: For sheer gall you get the prize for coming here now when just a short time ago in front of Miss Ryan you made it abundantly clear you didn't like me and made insinuations and accusations about me which were unfounded and untrue. Well, I'm still that same person, Mr. Horn, and now you come yelping like the injured party. *There's* the injured party, Mr. Horn!" Van Zeider pointed to Emile. "And I'm still that same person you don't like — not red, yellow, black, or blue, but *white*. I take pride in that whiteness, and I don't give a fig for the Apache Kid or the rest of those inferiors penned up with him. Miles can ship them to Florida or to hell. I only wish the both of you were going with them. Good day, *gentlemen*."

"Yeah, good day, Van Zeider," Horn said, "but there'll be another day."

"If that's a threat, pardon me for not trembling," Van Zeider replied.

"Come on, Tom," Sieber urged. "Let's get outta here before I do something permanent." The two scouts wheeled and walked out.

Karl Van Zeider cackled audibly as they left.

"I wouldn't laugh at them two," Emile warned his brother, taking another drink. "I just wouldn't."

"When I need or want your advice, dear brother, I'll ask loudly and clearly."

"Sure, sure, Karl. You're the boss."

"Thank you for the reassurance."

"But ask or no, I'll tell you this: I think what you got set up tonight is a mistake.

You're taking a chance of —"

"I'm taking no chance whatsoever. There's no way we can be linked to Geronimo's . . . shall we say, dash for freedom."

"But why help him bust out?"

"Because I have use for him a little longer in these parts. You have to admit that up to now he's been *very* useful."

"Yeah, but suppose they kill him while he's trying to bust loose?"

"Suppose they do?" Karl Van Zeider smiled. "We'll be no worse off than if he were away. I'm not sure he'd be either."

"I guess you're right." Emile shrugged.

"Quit guessing, Emile, and let me do the brainwork." Van Zeider pointed to the nearly empty whiskey bottle. "And go easy on that. We're supposed to sell it, not swill it."

Chapter 15

Horn lay on the cot in the quarters he shared with Sieber and the Kid. Sieber stretched out in the cot across the room. The third bunk was empty. Years ago Sieber had appropriated an adobe structure for himself and his sons. The adobe was composed of two rooms, each sixteen feet square. Each had an earth floor and three windows with four small glass panes each. The first room served as a combination parlor-kitchen. The three scouts slept in the other room whenever they were at Fort Bowie. More often, they slept in the desert or the mountains under the naked sky.

Horn had picked up the Apache Kid's knife on the way out of Doctor Barnes's waiting room. A glint of moonlight through the window reflected on the blade as Horn turned it by the hilt in his hand. He rose from the cot and walked toward the west window.

"Al, you ever see an Apache get his day in court?"

"What're you saying?" Sieber did not stir from his bunk. Horn knew that the old scout's rheumatism had bunched up on him.

"I'm saying maybe we ought to bust the Kid out of there."

"You off your feed?" Sieber croaked.

"Maybe we'll hear from Crook, and maybe we won't. He doesn't have any authority around here anyhow. All he can do is recommend. Miles'll just use that recommendation to light one of his cigars."

"Not if the recommendation comes from Sherman or Sheridan."

"Army channels take time, too much time — probably more than the Kid's got before they haul him out of here. And I know the governor's your friend, but I'm not sure this is a civilian matter, and neither are you. It's all right to try to boost the Kid's spirits, but between you and me, I don't think he's got any more chance than a wax cat in hell."

"You could be right about that."

"I been in jail a couple times myself. I know what it'll be like for him."

"So?"

"So, maybe we ought to bust him out."

"Tom, you're a bright young fella, but sometimes I think your brains are on vacation. Even if we wanted to, how in the hell could we do it? He's not inside some goddamn plum pudding. That jail's made out of stone and iron, with locks, and guarded by friends of ours. You think they'll just look the other way? Or you figure on shootin 'em down?"

"There's got to be a way."

"Even if he did get out, you know what it'd be like for him to be a wanted man the rest of his life?"

"Better than that swamp — and Geronimo."

"Besides, we couldn't get him out of there without being recognized ourselves. Hell, Miles'd be after *our* asses too. No. We got to do it legal, and you know it."

"Yeah, I know it. But I just had to say it anyhow."

"Well, now that you said it, forget it."

Horn walked back toward his bunk. He stuck the knife into the table in the center of the room. There was a whiskey bottle on the table — an empty whiskey bottle.

"I'm going out," said Horn. "Want to come along?"

"Where?"

"Do some drinking — and thinking. You coming?"

"Nope."

A nighthawk sounded through the dark-

129

ness as Tom Horn walked past the bare flagpole in the center of Fort Bowie's compound. Like all the forts in the territory, Fort Bowie had been built since the Civil War. When fighting broke out between the states the United States Army troopers were ordered to withdraw from Arizona and participate in the internecine slaughter. Some of those troopers traded in their blue uniforms for gray before going about the business of bloodletting.

But when the troops withdrew, they were ordered to dismantle or burn all the forts in the territory so they could not be used by the Apaches against the white miners, settlers, cowboys and ranchers.

Most of the white population left the meadows, deserts, and ranches and fled to the larger towns, which afforded them protection from the rampant natives.

After the "secession" question was settled by bloodbath, the army reentered the Arizona Territory and built new forts at Bowie, Whipple, Defiance, Apache, Lowell, and other bastions of defense and offense to settle the "redskin" question. Most of those redskins were Apaches.

There were seven thousand Apaches when the Cochise War broke out. In ten years the American government spent more than thirty-eight million dollars to exterminate the Apache population. During that campaign seven thousand *one hundred* survived. The Indians succeeded in reproducing faster than the United States Army could reduce them.

Of those original seven thousand Apaches, only two thousand were fighting men. The other five thousand were women and children or old men too feeble to fight.

But the government policy helped defeat itself, because in reality there were two policies working at cross purposes. The Department of Interior's intention was to protect the Apaches, but the War Department, through its army, vowed to exterminate those same Apaches.

No one succeeded in explaining all this to the Indians who had lived here hundreds of years under the curious notion that this was their land. When the United States acquired almost fifty thousand square miles from Mexico for ten million dollars, under the Gadsen Purchase of 1853, no one sat down and talked about the deal to the seven thousand Apaches who populated the territory.

The Apaches had never acknowledged the sovereignty of either Mexico or Spain, and now they had to bargain with the

Americans over their own property rights. So the United States government, feeling a mite guilty about these troublesome natives, fed and penned them with one hand while trying to shoot them dead with the other.

Meanwhile, a lot of people — not Apaches — got rich, and the railroad came through.

Tom Horn reflected on all this as he headed toward Van Zeider's *cantina*. He noted that the lamps in Ryan's store were all out. He imagined that Shana Ryan was probably asleep in the small apartment behind the store, in the room where he and Tim had sometimes sat through most of the night and talked about the future of the West. And now Shana Ryan slept in that room. Tom thought of her long, flowing flaxen hair. Then he made his mind drift in a different direction, toward Van Zeider's *cantina,* where the lamps were still lit.

But Shana Ryan was not in bed. She stood in the darkness of the store and watched Tom Horn's strong silhouette moving away from her through the placid spring night.

It was almost midnight when Horn entered the open door of the *cantina.* Some of

132

the damage still showed. The window had been repaired, but the broken mirror had not been replaced. Most of the soldiers had turned in a long time ago, but five were still there playing poker at a far table. There was another game going on with four civilian participants.

The same bald-headed, bow-legged old coot who had acted as messenger was leaning on the bar talking to Peg until Horn stepped in. They stopped talking. Everyone stopped talking.

Horn took two more steps, wiped his mouth, and looked directly at Peg, who didn't know what to do or say.

"Evening, Peg," said Horn. "You can leave that scattergun just where it rests."

"Yes, sir," said Peg. "Look, Mr. Horn, I'm just a poor, one-legged bartender trying to make a living."

"Who said otherwise?" Horn replied.

"Just remember that," Peg said, then hollered out toward the back room, "Mr. Van Zeider!"

Tom Horn stood waiting.

The door opened, and Karl Van Zeider walked through, then stopped at the sight of Horn. But Van Zeider collected himself quickly. He smoothly fingered the fob at his vest. "Look here, Mr. Horn," Van

Zeider said firmly, "I don't want any more trouble around here."

Horn took a step forward and said nothing.

"I don't want to have to send for the army," Van Zeider warned.

"Don't worry, Van Zeider," Horn said. "You won't have to send for the army . . . or the marines." He took another step closer. "I just want you to take a good look at me. Go ahead and look."

"What for?" Van Zeider asked uncertainly.

"To make sure."

"Of what?"

Horn let the moment hang.

"That I'm not an Indian," he answered at last.

"What?" Van Zeider laughed.

"Look! Look and make sure. Am I an Indian?"

Karl Van Zeider looked at Horn for a moment; then his eyes swept to the card players, then across to Peg and back to Horn.

"No. You're not an Indian," Van Zeider affirmed.

"Good," Horn nodded. "Can a non-Indian buy a drink in this place?"

"Why, yes. Sure." Van Zeider relaxed

and smiled. "Sure! Peg, give Mr. Horn a drink. Give him all the drinks he wants to buy. His money's just as good as any other white man's. Make yourself comfortable, Mr. Horn, but you'll have to excuse me." Van Zeider nodded toward the back room. "I've got some bookkeeping to take care of. Good night, gentlemen."

Van Zeider turned briskly, walked through the back-room door, then closed and locked it.

Horn moved to the bar. The old coot took a step to the side, giving Horn some more room, even though he had more than he needed. Horn reached in his pocket and put money on the bar. Peg produced a bottle and placed a whiskey glass beside it.

Horn took the bottle, bit off the cork, and spat it away.

"We won't need that," he said. "And Peg, bring up a bigger glass."

"Sure thing, Mr. Horn," Peg said, and brought up a tumbler. "How's this?"

"Just about right." Horn picked up the bottle and the glass and walked away from the bar. "I'll sit at my usual table."

Horn went to the window table at which Sieber, Crane, and the Apache Kid had sat, settled in a chair, and poured whiskey into the tumbler until it was half-full.

Horn drank.

Half an hour later the soldiers broke up their poker game and left.

Horn drank.

In another half hour the four civilians cashed in their game and filed out.

Horn drank.

Outside under a star-spilled sky, the Fort lay quiet like a becalmed solitary ship at sea.

Horn drank.

In the back room, Karl Van Zeider whispered to one of his teamsters, Pete Curtain. Curtain had participated along with Emile in the fracas that led to Emile's hospitalization.

"Everything set?" Van Zeider inquired.

"Yep. Dynamite, wagon, rifles, and two of Geronimo's bucks fresh off San Carlos. But I don't think they got a Chinaman's chance."

"Another thinker," Van Zeider said almost to himself.

"You said what?" Pete Curtain inquired.

"I said there's the door." Van Zeider pointed to the door leading to the back alleyway.

When Curtain left, Van Zeider removed the gold watch from his vest pocket and thumbed open the hunting case. It was exactly 1:00 A.M.

Tom Horn stared at the empty whiskey bottle on the table. He had consumed its contents, all but the couple of ounces of fiery fluid still in the tumbler he held in his right hand. The whiskey burning in his belly and brain did nothing to sort out and settle the problems he, Sieber, and the Apache Kid had — especially the Kid.

He thought to himself. All the whiskey in the world won't justify God's ways to man — or man's ways to man.

"Beg pardon, Mr. Horn." Peg limped a couple of steps down the bar closer to Horn. "But it's time."

"What?"

"It's time to go."

"Where?"

"I mean, we're closing up." Peg wiped the top of the battered bar with a towel.

Horn looked around the room and saw that it was empty. Even the old coot had taken leave. Horn thought, I must have been somewhere else, all right. Didn't even notice Baldy when he left.

"All right, Peg, ol' partner." Horn rose, finished off the tumbler, walked to the bar, and put money there. "That's good whiskey. It'd turn the devil against sin. Better give me one for the road, friend

Peg — one bottle."

"Yes, sir." The amputee produced another bottle and placed it near the money.

"Well," said Horn, taking the bottle and walking toward the door, "I think I'll go out and talk to a hooty owl. They're wise old birds, those hooty owls. Maybe I can find me one and talk to him. Wise old owl might know the answers, 'cause I sure as hell don't, and neither do you — do you, old friend Peg?"

"No, sir, Mr. Horn. I sure as hell don't."

Bottle in hand, Horn walked out of the *cantina* and breathed deep of the warm, thin air. Fort Bowie was quiet, at peace. Miles hadn't even posted sentries.

The war was over.

"God's in his heaven," Horn half-whispered to himself. "All the Apaches penned up — and all's right with the world. But I got to find me a hooty owl." He walked along the building until he came to Ryan's store. Horn pulled the cork from the bottle and looked into the stem. He brought the bottle up close to his right eye. "Hello, hooty owl. I know you're in there. Come on out and talk to me. I got to ask you some questions. Playing it cagey, huh? Well, I know how to get you out."

Horn put the bottle to his mouth and

drank. Then he placed one hand against a post and leaned over to vomit. He tried. Nothing came up, but the attempt made him dizzy and weak. He raised the bottle toward his face again.

"Hooty owl, I'm coming in after you. . . ."

"Tom, are you all right?" Shana Ryan opened the door and stood with a robe around her nightclothes. "Tom?"

"First-rate." Horn's words slurred just a little. "I am first-rate, Miz Shana."

"Who are you talking to?" Shana smiled.

"I'm talking to the wise old hooty owl," Horn said, holding up the bottle, "but he won't come out and talk to me."

"Oh, yes, of course." Shana nodded. "I see. I also think you better come inside. I'll heat the coffeepot." She reached a hand to Horn's arm and guided him through the door.

They made their way through the dark store and into the apartment.

"You think that old hooty owl might be in the coffeepot?" asked Tom.

"He might be." Shana directed Horn to a couch, and he sat.

In a few minutes he had a hot mug of coffee in his hand. "I set out to find a hooty owl," said Horn, still showing the effects of the whiskey he had gone up against, "and instead I found a bird of paradise. Miz Shana, you are purely a bird of paradise."

"And you, Mr. Horn, better have another cup of coffee." Shana poured from the pot into the mug in Horn's hand. When she walked to replace the pot on top of the stove, Horn laced the brew with a double shot of whiskey from his bottle. Shana observed him and smiled. "It's customary to add a little sugar or cream."

"Different tribes, different customs." Horn drank the hot fluid from the mug with an amazingly steady hand and looked at Shana Ryan.

She wore no makeup. And though she was just as covered as if she were wearing a dress, there was something about the sight of this beautiful woman in her nightclothes that betrayed a heretofore unacknowledged intimacy between them. Part of it was the way her silken hair fell in unstudied waves over her shoulders and rested softly on her breasts. Part of it was her surprisingly small slippered feet. And part of it was that unmistakably sensual nocturnal look in her wide-set eyes. Tom Horn remembered how he had thought of her that night just before the attack on the Apache village, wondering if he would ever see her again. And now here they were alone at night in a warm and private place.

"Would you like me to fix you a couple of eggs to go with that coffee?" Shana asked. "It'll only take a few minutes."

"No, thanks," Horn said, then added, "You're a good woman."

"Thank you."

"And your brother was a good man." Horn was by no means sober yet. "So's Al Sieber, a good man . . . and Captain Melvyn Crane, and General Nelson Appleton Miles is a good man . . . and everybody . . . but the Apache Kid. He ain't no good. You see, he's an Indian . . . so" — Horn took a deep gulp from the mug — "we're gonna send the Apache Kid away . . . with all the other bad Indians to some place where we won't have to worry about 'em no more. . . ."

Unconsciously, Horn's thumb and forefinger were rubbing the talon at his throat.

Shana pointed. "May I ask what that is you wear around your neck?"

"Oh, it's just . . . just an eagle claw."

"I noticed Mr. Sieber and the Apache Kid also —"

"Yeah," Horn interrupted. "Al gave 'em to us when he said we were . . . well, he gave 'em to us some time back."

"One of the men here told me that Mr. Sieber raised the Apache Kid."

"From a pup."

"And you, too?"

"I was some older when I got to know Al . . . but he taught us both, like his own sons."

"In a way that makes you and the Apache Kid sort of brothers, doesn't it?"

"No. It don't." Horn paused. "But we are." He set the mug down. His head had become heavy, his eyes weary. He leaned his head back on the couch. "Funny — my brother's an Indian . . . and I'm not."

Tom Horn closed his eyes.

Geronimo's eyes were open.

In a few minutes it would be 2:00 A.M. Geronimo had no watch, but he knew what time it was.

He stood near the bars and looked across the darkness at the unmoving figure of the Apache Kid, lying in the opposite cell. Each of the other cells held two and some even three Indian prisoners. Only Geronimo and the Kid had private accommodations, such as they were.

The long, narrow chamber had been sectioned off into a dozen small cells on each side. The cells were now dark and quiet

142

except for the intermittent snoring of some restive brave. At the end of the north side were the guards' quarters. Two soldiers, Sergeant Edward Krantz and Private Slim Dawson, were on duty that night. They weren't expected to remain awake, and they didn't. Sergeant Krantz, the ranking trooper, slept on a cot, while Dawson made do in a chair.

Outside, the night sank into its deepest darkness, and in that darkness a figure skulked toward the west wall of the guardhouse. He was a young Apache brave named Mandan, dressed in a dirty, ill-fitting United States Cavalry uniform consisting of kepi, tunic, and trousers — but Mandan still wore the soft, silent moccasins of the Apache. Mandan had a pistol in his holster, another gun was tucked in his belt, and he carried three sticks of dynamite lashed together and with a six-inch wick.

Fifty yards farther out in the darkness, another Apache buck named Chukra sat on a wagon hitched to a pair of strong, fast horses. Chukra was also dressed in what passed for a United States Cavalry uniform in the dark. Near his knees were two Winchesters, loaded.

Mandan reached a spot below one of the windows of the guardhouse. A bird call came from between his thin lips.

From inside the cell, a bird named Geronimo answered the call.

Mandan placed the dynamite at the base of Geronimo's cell, lit the fuse, ran as fast as he could along the wall for about thirty feet, then flattened himself against it.

Inside, Geronimo was braced in a corner farthest from the exposed outer wall.

The explosion went off, and the wall blew away as if it had been hit by a cannonball.

Every Indian in the guardhouse, including the Apache Kid, bolted to his feet.

All but the Kid and Geronimo began yelping, screaming, and chanting. In the guardroom, Sergeant Krantz leaped up and Dawson fell from the tilted chair onto the earthen floor.

At the sound of the discharge, Chukra lashed the horses, and the wagon rattled toward the blown-out wall.

Mandan appeared at the newly made opening and tossed Geronimo a pistol. Encumbered by the heavy leg irons, Geronimo turned and fired the pistol at the Apache Kid's cell.

The Kid dived into a corner behind the bunk. Geronimo fired again and again. Two of the shots hit the iron bars in the

Kid's cell; the rest ripped and ricocheted around his hunched-up body.

The wagon clattered to a stop at the opening, and Mandan yelled for Geronimo to hurry. Geronimo threw the empty pistol at the Kid's cell and clanked through the hole in the wall. Mandan helped the chief onto the wagon just as Krantz and Dawson appeared at Geronimo's cell and fired their pistols toward the fleeing Apaches.

"Geronimo!" Krantz yelled to everyone and no one. "It's Geronimo! He got loose! He's escaping!"

Dawson ran down the long, ghostly corridor toward the outside to rouse the fort.

But the fort was already roused. The dynamite and gunshots had done that well enough. Soldiers and civilians alike thought Fort Bowie was under siege. Soldiers and civilians, blasted out of tranquil slumber, were grabbing rifles and guns and, still in night clothes, some nearly naked, were running about to defend their lives and fortunes. Somewhere a bugle sounded assembly.

But Tom Horn had a head start.

Except for his hat, he was already dressed and armed on the porch of Ryan's store. At the sound of the explosion, he had sprung awake. Shana had been in her room asleep. Horn ran through the apartment and the store and tore open the front door.

Now Horn stood on the porch, pistol in hand, and watched the wagon roaring flat out in his direction and toward the vast black night below the fort. It looked as if a trooper were at the reins and another next to him, but even in the darkness, Horn recognized the unmistakable figure of Geronimo standing in the bed of the wagon, firing a Winchester at some scurrying soldiers.

Wherever that wagon was heading, Horn would make sure it wouldn't get there.

Horn shot the horse nearest him. The animal screamed, tumbled in its traces, and fell dead, taking the other horse down with him and tipping over the wagon. The wagon rolled twice, throwing off the three Indians, then thumped to a dusty stop with all four wheels spinning in the air.

Mandan was first to his feet. He fired toward Horn. Just as the bullet shattered the store window behind him, Horn took aim at the exposed Indian. Horn's slug tore through Mandan's throat.

Chukra was on one knee, also in the open. His pistol went off three times before two of Horn's bullets dropped him.

Geronimo, dazed by the fall and hampered by the chains, crawled on his elbows and knees toward the fallen Winchester. He reached it just as Horn arrived to kick the rifle out of Geronimo's grasp.

Once again the old warrior looked up into the barrel of Tom Horn's gun.

A crowd consisting of nearly everyone in the fort converged around Horn and Geronimo.

If General Nelson Appleton Miles looked ridiculous in his white-plumed hat, he looked even more ridiculous without it in his stocking feet, military tunic, and underwear. The sword he held in his hand completed the effect.

They were all there — Sieber, Shana, Crane, Karl Van Zeider, Pete Curtain, Doctor Barnes, Nurse Thatcher, Baldy, and even Peg.

"By heaven!" Miles roared at Horn. "How did this red devil get out of that guardhouse?"

"Don't ask me, General — I'm retired." Horn pointed to Geronimo. "Ask him. But I don't think he'll tell you."

Doctor Barnes walked over. He had just finished examining Mandan and Chukra.

"Those other two aren't going to be telling any more lies or having any more

147

breakfasts. Tom, you shoot better by dark than by daylight."

"Just aimed at the sound of their guns," said Horn.

"Yeah, well, one of 'em must of had his gun in his throat." Barnes glanced at Nurse Thatcher, who in her nightgown resembled a fugitive scarecrow. "Come on, Nurse Hatchet. Those poor souls are beyond any harm you can do them."

"Captain Crane," Miles commanded, pointing his sword toward Geronimo, "I want this man handcuffed. And make arrangements to have him and the rest of his savages shipped out by Monday."

"Just a minute, General." Doctor Barnes had overheard Miles and turned back. "Monday's only four days from now. Some of those people are sick and wounded. They're not fit to travel yet."

"Fit or unfit, every damn one of them is going to be on that train out of here on Monday. Is that clear, Captain?"

"Yes, sir," Crane responded.

"Good night." Miles reflexively started to sheath his sword, until he realized that there was no scabbard attached to his underpants. Sword in hand, he headed toward his quarters.

Geronimo's eyes burned into Horn. He

said nothing as Crane and six troopers led him back to the guardhouse.

"Tom?" Shana Ryan put her hand on Horn's arm. "Are you all right?"

Horn smiled and nodded.

"Tom, are you coming?" Sieber asked.

"Yeah, I'm coming."

"Very fortunate, Mr. Horn," Van Zeider intoned.

"What's fortunate?"

"Why, the fact that you were near this particular spot so late at night — or early in the morning." Van Zeider looked with implication from Ryan's store to Shana to Horn.

The muscles in Horn's neck tensed, and he started to move a step toward Van Zeider, but Shana's hand squeezed his arm even tighter.

"Well good night, everybody." Van Zeider hooked both thumbs into his vest and walked away.

"I'm gonna get some sleep if it kills me," said Sieber, and moved in the opposite direction.

"Tom," Shana whispered, even though the two of them stood alone in the darkness, "you left your hat inside." She smiled.

"I know," said Horn. "And my bottle. Gives me an excuse to come by tomorrow."

Chapter 16

By the first light of sunrise, Horn and Sieber walked toward Sieber's horse, which was already saddled and ready to ride. Sieber would get to Globe by horseback and take the overnight stage to Prescott. With any luck, he'd be back in Bowie before Monday. Of course, it might take Governor C. Meyer Zulick longer than that to reach a decision in the matter. Governor Zulick was not an impulsive man. He had to be sure of his legal footing before treading a tightrope.

Sieber did his best to work the morning stiffness out of his legs and back. He bent from one side to the other, arched his spine, hinged up one knee then the other. He took hold of the pommel, worked his boot into the loop of the stirrup, and levered his body onto the saddle.

"Well, Al," Horn said, "use them spurs."

"I intend to." Sieber patted the mane of his horse.

"No. I mean on your friend — Lead Ass Zulick."

"I'll do what I can, but he's awful set in his ways. You know how cautious them

150

lawyers are. Say, where's your hat?"

"Huh? Oh, I . . . I musta lost it last night."

"You better go look for it. That's a good hat. Well, tell the Kid I'll do what I can. *Auf Wiedersehen.*"

"*Adiós,* Al."

Still hatless, Tom Horn opened the door to the guardhouse and walked in. Even though Krantz and Dawson were no longer on duty, they were still in the guards' quarters drinking coffee, along with Sergeant Pat Cahill and trooper Dennis Ward, who had relieved them a few minutes ago.

"Mornin', Tom," Krantz greeted, lifting a cup. "Care for some tar? Fresh made."

"No, thanks."

"Look, Tom," Krantz went on, "me and Dawson here didn't get a chance to thank you last night. We thought it wise to stay outta General Miles' sightlines before he started askin' too many how's, why's, and wherefore's, but you pulled our butts outta the burner. Did Geronimo get away, ol' Miles mighta had us shot. So . . . well, thanks."

"Forget it," Horn answered.

"Geronimo won't forget it," Sergeant Cahill said. "That was his last hurrah. He's

151

got more iron on him than a kitchen stove."

"Can I go back there and talk to the Kid?" Horn nodded toward the cellblock.

"You bet," Cahill smiled, "so long as Dennis here goes back part ways with you. Those Apaches'd sooner peel your hide than anything I can think of."

"Thanks." Horn started toward the cellblock.

"Oh, and Tom . . ." Cahill almost winced. "We had to cuff the Kid, too — orders."

There was a lethal silence as Horn walked the long corridor bisecting the cellblock. Every cold, black Apache eye followed his every step. Hate hung thick as paste in the stillness.

As Horn passed, Geronimo's eyes were twin vials of venom. He had been moved three cells toward the guardroom. Two other Apaches had been evicted and transferred into another chamber so Geronimo still possessed private accommodations. He also possessed a set of handcuffs. Rather, they possessed him.

Horn stopped and looked at the dynamited cell a moment, then turned to the Apache Kid, who stood by the iron bars.

"Howdy, Kid."

For answer the Apache Kid brought up

to his chest both fists bound by the iron handcuffs.

"Yeah, I know." Horn bit his lip. "Look, Kid, Miles is fixing to ship you and . . . the rest of 'em out of here on Monday. . . ." Horn stopped and looked into the Kid's eyes. "You already knew, didn't you?"

The Kid nodded slightly.

"*How* did you know? Did the guards tell you?"

"No. I just knew. Remember, I'm an Indian."

"Al's already on his way to Prescott. We hope to get word before then."

"Tom, it's no use. I'll do what I have to."

"Now, don't try anything dumb, Kid." Horn motioned toward the hole in the opposite cell. "He tried and didn't get very far."

"If I did break out, would you come after me, Tom, like you did him?"

"What kind of talk is that? You know better, you know that I —"

"I know," the Kid answered.

"Ol' Geronimo had some help," Horn changed the subject, glanced again at the blown-out cell. "Dynamite, horses, wagon, and Winchesters — white man's help."

The Kid nodded in agreement.

"You'll have help too, Kid — but a different kind. We'll do it legal." Horn pulled a pouch out of his breast pocket. "Here's tobacco and the makings. I'll be back."

"*Skookum*," said the Kid, and took the pouch with his manacled hands, then motioned to Horn's head. "Where's your hat?"

"Huh? Oh, I musta left it back in the room. Well, see you, Kid."

Horn turned and without looking in either direction started to walk toward trooper Dennis Ward, who waited halfway up the corridor.

If it began by signal, the signal was unseen and unheard. As Horn took his first step he listened to a low, plaintive wail. It came from the mouth of every penned-up Apache in the guardhouse except for Geronimo and the Kid. Horn had heard it before — the knell of death, the mysterious but unmistakable dirge to the dead. Tom Horn knew that the litany was for him. But it was not a lamentation; it was a celebration, a chant celebrating the death of an enemy — Tom Horn.

Shana Ryan was dragging a bushel of potatoes when Tom Horn walked into the store.

"Good morning, Tom."

154

"Morning. Here, let me do that. Where do you want it?"

"Over there." Shana pointed to a pile of groceries by the counter. "I'm getting an order ready for the Chandlers."

"What you ought to get is some help around here."

"I had some. But after payday he decided to get drunk. Haven't seen him since," she smiled.

"Speaking of drink . . ." Horn cleared his throat. "I want to thank you for what you did last night and to apologize —"

"No apology necessary. You were a perfect gentleman."

"At one in the morning? With a snootful? It's a good thing you take in strays."

"I'm very particular about the 'strays' I take in, Mr. Horn. But this fellow said he was looking for a hooty owl, and . . ."

"Yes, ma'am. I remember. And some of the other things I said, well . . ."

"You were very nice. I've never been called a bird of paradise before. I suppose you've come for your whiskey and your hat."

"Just as soon leave the whiskey here, but I never knew so many people noticed a hat before."

155

"Follow me," Shana said, leading the way toward the apartment. "I thought it best not to bring it out here, just in case some curious customer started asking questions about it."

"Like that Van Zeider? I didn't like what he said last night and the way he said it."

"There's not much about Karl Van Zeider that you do approve of." Shana handed Horn his hat.

"Let's put it this way" — Horn adjusted the hat on his head to its accustomed angle — "if he don't go to hell, there's no use having one. Well, thanks."

Horn extended his hand. Shana fitted her palm into his. Tom's was a big hand, hard and used to the feel of reins, the curve of a pistol, and the metal and wood of a Winchester — a hand that had dealt death. Still, there were warmth and tenderness to its touch. For an instant Shana felt safe and secure. She had thought about him last night as she lay in her bed — how awkward and almost childlike he seemed, loyal and concerned about his friend the Apache Kid . . . questioning the inequities of man's inequities to man. He was shy and considerate — and then the change outside, with a gun in this same hand. He had stood nerveless, defiant in death's

156

doorway, shooting the horse and, with bullets flying at him, killing two men and kicking the rifle out of Geronimo's grasp.

He was a changeable man, this Tom Horn, whom she had met only a short time ago — a sudden man. But he had warmth and a tender touch. Reluctantly, she took her hand from his.

"Can I help you with the rest of that order out there?" he asked.

"I'm sure the Chandlers would be very pleased," Shana smiled, "and I would too."

"So would I," Tom Horn said, and gently touched the tips of his fingers to the flesh of her forearm as they walked from the apartment into the store.

Chapter 17

At noon on Monday, a steaming locomotive pointing east, coupled to two cars and a caboose, waited on the tracks near the depot where a large platform festooned with red, white, and blue streamers had been set up for the celebration.

It would be an event to remember, a historical highlight in the short but sanguine saga of the Arizona Territory. Soon Geronimo and the shackled remnants of his brigade, along with the women, wounded, and children of his tribe, would be loaded like cattle and exiled forever from their homeland.

The order went down from General Miles that every trooper would wear a clean uniform and polished buckles, buttons, and boots.

Hundreds of citizens converged from many miles to cast a final look at Geronimo, the scourge of the territory, and to participate in a ceremonial tribute to the territory's great liberator General Nelson Appleton Miles.

Even throughout this last hour, Doctor

Barnes and Nurse Thatcher circulated among the infirm and wounded Apaches who had been herded to the depot. Some of the Indians were too sick or weak to stand. Up to almost the last minute, doctor and nurse changed bandages and dispensed drugs to the dazed and bewildered Chiricahuas.

A brass band struck up "The Battle Hymn of the Republic" while dozens of white children who had been excused from school that day scampered among the attending adults. Dogs barked at the music, and stray chickens clucked in accompaniment.

A good time was being had by most — not by Tom Horn nor by Al Sieber, who had ridden in less than an hour ago and who showed the effects of his journey. Sieber didn't wait for a stagecoach to come back; he'd made the trip on horseback. What little sleep he did get was in the saddle. And now Horn and Sieber were making their way toward the Apache Kid, who stood handcuffed with the other prisoners.

"Kid," said Horn, "Al just got back. Wore down a dozen fat horses doing it."

"The governor's studying your case," Sieber said wearily. "He promised he'd do everything he could."

"But," Horn had to add, "it's gonna take a while."

"He better hurry," the Kid said bitterly. "I got a train to catch."

Just then, at a signal from Mr. Noah Mumford, chairman of the presentation committee, the band struck up a fanfare. Noah Mumford, along with several other prominent citizens, including Karl Van Zeider, stood on the raised and decorated platform with Nelson Appleton Miles, whose brass buttons and buckles shone in the noon sun. Another signal from Mumford finished off the fanfare.

One of the other committeemen stepped forward and handed Mumford an ornately engraved gold sword. Noah Mumford nodded, turned to General Miles, nodded again, faced the assembly, and cleared his throat.

"General Miles . . ." Mumford cleared his throat once more. "It is with deep gratitude that the good citizens of the territory present you with this here gold sword." Mumford held the sword by the hilt, tip toward the sun, for all the crowd to consider. He held it there until he thought the crowd had considered it enough, then went on, "This sword is given in appreciation of what you've done since you come here, and not too long ago at that. But you got the job done, and that's the point of the whole matter."

Noah Mumford looked around in expectation of applause. After a short wait there was some polite hand-clapping, led by Karl Van Zeider. Mumford took the opportunity to clear his throat again.

"We're sure this territory, including the San Carlos Reservation, will be a better and safer place to live and work and raise our kids now that we're gonna get rid of . . ." Noah Mumford paused and then dramatically pointed directly at Geronimo. ". . . them there hostiles."

Mumford surrendered the sword to General Miles, who bowed slightly and raised the weapon in benediction as the onlookers applauded.

"Didn't take 'em long to forget about Crook," said Sieber, not applauding.

"I don't know," Horn answered. "Rumor is, the good citizens didn't come up with enough money for that there cutlass and the general himself ponied up the difference."

The general himself held up a hand, signaling for an end to the already diminished applause so he might commence his remarks.

161

"Mr. Mumford, Mr. Van Zeider, distinguished citizens, and men of my command: I accept this honor and will treasure it among my most esteemed trophies. For years you have endured the costly, bloody, and unprovoked attacks by recalcitrant renegades whom this government has sought to reform and redeem.

"I am convinced that there can be no permanent peace and security in this part of our great nation except in one way — namely, the capture and complete disarmament of the hostiles and their removal beyond, far beyond, the limit of your territory.

"When this train pulls out, that is what I will have accomplished. I thank you."

Once again Miles hoisted the sword in the air, and once again the collected citizens applauded. This time the locomotive engineer punctuated the applause with a couple of toots from the train whistle.

Throughout the ceremony Geronimo, though fettered hand and foot, seemed fiercely unsubdued, as if his mind and eyes were unattached to his manacled body — as if his real self were still riding free with the spring wind in the mesas and mountains, plotting revenge on those who would rob him of his freedom. Geronimo held nothing but petty contempt for the fat-necked general who strutted about with his plumed hat and gold sword. Geronimo would gladly face a hundred such enemies — five hundred — in preference to the three enemies he looked upon now: Sieber, Horn, and the Kid.

At least the Kid would be within reach. And somehow Geronimo would reach out and kill him. There would be other Apaches who would revenge themselves on Sieber and Horn.

A nod from General Miles and the loading process began. The braves were herded into the forward car. The women, two of whom were pregnant, the children and the wounded were deployed to the rear.

Captain Crane made his way alongside Horn and Sieber, who walked with the Apache Kid.

"I'm sorry." Crane looked into the Kid's eyes and repeated, "I'm sorry," then quickly walked away.

One of the soldiers took the Kid's arm and pushed him toward the rear car with the women. "You get special treatment," the soldier snapped, "back there with the squaws."

"Take it easy, Kid," Horn said. "Don't

do anything foolish."

The Apache Kid didn't look back. He walked aboard the second car with the women and children.

The train whistle sounded again, and hot white steam poured from the engine.

Doctor Jedadiah Barnes and Nurse Thatcher now stepped near Horn and Sieber. There were the beginnings of tears in the nurse's tired eyes. The doctor pulled out an already sweat-soaked handkerchief and wiped his wet face.

"This is a black day," Barnes said. "A black day. I begged Miles to let some of those people stay behind. There's a half dozen near dead. Might just as well ship 'em in coffins. *Begged* him, but he wouldn't listen. Hell, one of them women's so ready she's liable to drop that papoose before they hit the border. Well, come on, Hatchet — let's get a move on. I've seen and heard enough around here to make me bilious for a month. Say, what the hell's a matter with you, anyway?"

"I've got a cinder in my eye, you old skeleton maker!" Nurse Thatcher knuckled a tear away from her bony face. "That's what's a matter with me."

"A black day," Doctor Jedadiah Barnes

repeated as he and Nurse Thatcher walked away.

The band struck up a chorus of "Auld Lang Syne." Noah Mumford started to sing. He waved both arms and urged the crowd to join him.

They did.

Should old acquaintance be forgot,
And never brought to mind?
Should old acquaintance be forgot,
And days of auld lang syne!

The shiny iron wheels of the engine spun and scratched for traction. The locomotive hissed steam and shuddered. The train moved, and the couplings connecting the cars locked tight as the iron caravan crawled eastward.

For auld lang syne, my dear,
For auld lang syne . . .

Tom Horn and Al Sieber caught sight of the Apache Kid at a window. He had been manacled and deprived of his freedom. He had been arrested and convicted without judge or jury, sentenced without a hearing and exiled without appeal. He had been stripped of everything but the clothes he wore — and the eagle claw around his neck.

Horn turned to Sieber.

"You thinking what I'm thinking, Al?"

"I guess so."

"The Kid's got more steam in him than that boiler," Horn said. "I'm afraid of what he might do."

"So am I," Sieber nodded.

"Damn!"

The train gathered momentum, and so did the band and singers.

> We'll drink a cup of kindness yet,
> For days of auld lang syne.

Chapter 18

Later that afternoon the citizens and soldiers of Fort Bowie went back about their business. The platform was torn down. The chief beneficiaries of the proceedings were the schoolchildren. They got the entire day off and went about the fort playing cowboys and Indians.

Seth Barker, the homeliest boy — he was twelve — was conscripted to play Geronimo. Seth streaked mud across his face and found a worn-out broom to serve as a Winchester.

Luke Lipercott, who had achieved the venerable age of thirteen and already shaved once a week, was the logical choice to enact the role of Al Sieber, chief of scouts. The role of Tom Horn went to Sandy Bierce, since at age twelve he was the tallest of the young mummers. There was much yelling and shooting and ambushing, and finally Frank Lewis, also twelve, who had appropriated a cavalry bandana that served as his uniform, received a gold sword that formerly had been part of a wooden crate and made a speech almost as modest as General Miles's noon-time valediction to the hostiles.

Sieber went to his place to get a little sleep. In spite of his weariness, he knew he could sleep only in two- or three-hour spurts. Since he'd be up soon, he didn't bother taking off his clothes or boots. He did remove his hat and place it over his face. Ten seconds later Al Sieber was asleep.

General Miles supervised the mounting of his gold sword on a wall behind his desk. He instructed two troopers to tip the blade slightly upward to achieve an optimistic, victorious effect.

Miles stood a moment, studying the effect. He was pleased.

Tom Horn walked aimlessly around the fort. He visited his horse, Pilgrim, in the stable. Then he wandered some more. He thought about visiting the *cantina* and going up against some whiskey, but Karl Van Zeider might be there, and Horn had had more than enough of Van Zeider's society lately. After a while Tom Horn happened to wander aimlessly in the direction of Ryan's store.

Shana Ryan happened to be unloading a wagon marked VAN ZEIDER FREIGHTING hitched just in front of the store. She was struggling with a sack of flour. The sack was winning.

"Hello," said Horn.

"Hello, Tom."

"Just what do you think you're doing? Where's the teamster that delivered this load?"

Shana motioned toward the *cantina*. "He said he'd be right back, about a half hour ago. I needed some of these supplies to make up an order, so I thought . . ."

"You thought you'd hoist fifty-pound flour sacks?"

"I just need one for the order."

"Want me to go fetch him? Or would you rather I give you a hand?"

"I'd much prefer your hand," Shana smiled, "but at this rate I'm going to have to put you on the payroll."

"I'll settle for supper."

"Beef stew sound all right?"

"Sounds *skookum.*"

"What's *skookum?*"

"Indian for 'good,' 'great,' 'hallelujah!' "

"Well," she smiled, "I'll try to make that stew as *skookum* as I can."

As Tom Horn headed for the store carrying in his third load of supplies, Karl Van Zeider approached from the direction of Doctor Barnes's office-hospital. "You going into the grocery line, Mr. Horn?" Van Zeider inquired pleasantly.

"One of your teamsters is wetting his windpipe, so I'm just giving the lady a hand."

"I did hear the scouting business isn't so good lately," Van Zeider commented.

"That so?" Horn set the sack of flour against a bench on the porch. "And I hear the freighting business isn't going to be so good now that the railroad's come through."

"The secret of success in business is flexibility, Mr. Horn, and I pride myself on being very flexible."

"So's a snake."

"Look here, Horn — sometimes you exceed . . ." Van Zeider let the sentence go unfinished as Shana stepped out of the door.

"Good afternoon, Karl."

"Good afternoon." Van Zeider tipped his hat. "I didn't see you at the ceremony earlier today."

"No. I don't relish the sight of human beings bound in irons and sent away from their homes."

"I can appreciate that, Shana. But those renegades know nothing of humanity. They're wild animals, and we're all better

170

off without them. You'll understand someday."

"I hope not," Shana replied.

"Have you been thinking of my offer?"

"I'm still thinking, Karl."

"Well, it's still open, and you won't get a better one. If you'll excuse me, I'll leave you two to your . . . storekeeping." Van Zeider tipped his hat again and moved away.

"Flexible," Horn mumbled.

"What did you say, Tom?" Shana asked.

"Nothing worth repeating." Horn started to lift the flour sack from the bench.

"Tom! Hey, Tom! Hold up a minute." Sergeant Cahill was practically running across the compound, and with him were trooper Dennis Ward and Al Sieber. Cahill waved a fistful of money.

"Al," said Horn, "you up already?"

"You know I can only sleep in dribs and drabs. Besides, these two horse pestlers woke me up."

"Any word from the governor?" Horn asked.

Sieber shook his head. "Not yet."

"Tom, it's that time again." Sergeant Cahill held the money up. "We've collected over five hundred dollars to bet."

"That's more than last year," Horn noted.

"Well, hell, you won last year, didn't you? Oh!" Cahill turned to Shana. "Excuse me, ma'am, for the language."

"What the hell did he win?" Shana smiled.

"Biggest rodeo in Arizona, ma'am," Cahill beamed. "Being held in Globe. Last year ol' Tom set three world records and carried off a thousand dollars prize money. We're goin', ain't we, Tom?"

"Well . . ." Horn scratched behind his ear. "We sure could use that money, huh, Al?"

"Like a tick could use a furry place," said Sieber.

"Me and Dennis here got some leave coming. We'll ride along with you," Cahill volunteered.

"It'd be a week before we get back," Horn reflected, and looked at Sieber. "Don't think I ought to leave right now. I mean, the governor might . . ."

"You go ahead, Tom," Sieber said. "I'll stay here in case any word comes through. Win some of that prize money, boy."

"Well?" Cahill asked, looking at Horn. "Well?"

"Well," Horn said, "anybody want to

give me a hand with this load?"

"Me and Dennis'll do 'er, Tom. Come on, Dennis — don't just stand there like some dumb plow horse. Let's get to gettin'."

Doctor Jedadiah Barnes appeared from around a corner. "Tom!" The doctor was pumping for breath.

"Doc, what's wrong?" Horn asked. "Somebody dying?"

"Somebody's always dying. Don't mean anything's wrong." Doctor Barnes pulled money out of his vest pocket and handed it to Sergeant Cahill, then looked back at Horn. "I understand you're going rodeoing. Want the sergeant to bet fifteen dollars on you. That's all." Doctor Barnes wheeled and walked away, breathing even harder.

"Word sure does spread around here," Sieber observed.

"When we leaving, Tom?" Dennis Ward inquired.

"Well . . ." Horn looked at Shana. "I'm gonna have me some *skookum* supper and get a good night's sleep. We'll leave tomorrow by first light."

Horn and Shana sat at the kitchen table in her apartment, finishing dinner. The scout had taken a tub bath and changed into his suit. His Colt was still strapped on for ballast, but his freshly washed hair was parted in a straight line and scented with lilac water. During dinner he had loosened the black string tie that had been bowed at his throat.

Shana looked beautiful and fresh as a spring garden in a blue-and-yellow dress that matched her eyes and hair. She wore a blue ribbon at her throat with an ivory cameo pendant.

"You haven't said much, Tom."

"Too busy eating," Horn smiled.

"Skookum?" Shana pointed to his empty plate.

"Yes, ma'am. You're a good cook."

"Thank you."

"I'm a good cook myself."

"I'll bet you are."

"Have to be in the scouting business or go hungry most of the time."

"Is it true General Miles is . . . has . . . ?"

"Fired us scouts? It's true. He figures from now on it's going to be a more peaceable war."

"Have you been thinking about what you're going to do?"

"No, I guess not. Right now I've been thinking about something else. . . ."

"The Apache Kid?"

Horn nodded.

"You're doing everything possible, Tom. You and Mr. Sieber."

"Yeah, and the Kid's getting farther and farther away. Well, it sure was good stew."

"Would you like a drink from the hooty-owl whiskey bottle?"

"No, thanks."

"Well then" — Shana pointed to the oven — "how does fresh-baked apple pie sound?"

"Sounds good," said Horn. "Smells good too."

After the pie Shana walked Horn through the darkened store and to the front door.

"Can't recall a better dinner, drunk or sober," said Horn.

"You earned it," Shana smiled.

"Cahill and Dennis did most of the work."

"Tom?" Her face looked lovely, like the ivory white cameo at her throat framed in the moonlight, but soft and lambent. "You take care of yourself in Globe."

"I will." He nodded.

"And Tom, good luck and . . ." Her hands moved to his shoulders, her face floated close, and her lips touched his, just touched for a moment, then pressed warm and soft, unlike any lips Tom had kissed before. A feeling flashed through him, a feeling that had been unborn until that moonlit moment.

"Hurry back," she whispered.

"I will," said Horn. "You bet I will."

Tom Horn quietly eased into the room where Al Sieber slept. Without sound he pulled off his boots, took off his clothes, and laid them on a chair. He didn't bother to turn down the blanket. In his underclothes he silently slipped into the bed and looked out through a window at the mute spring moon.

"Anybody ever tell you," Sieber's voice drifted through the darkness, "that you smell real sweet?"

Chapter 19

Horn, Sergeant Cahill, and Trooper Ward rode northwest toward Globe.

The train, on its double silver path, headed due east, across the Arizona border toward the Pecos River that bisected the territory of New Mexico.

New Mexico, stepsister to Arizona and battleground of the Comanche Nation, whose warriors were the finest light cavalry in the history of mounted warfare.

New Mexico, where John Simpson Chisum drove ten thousand beeves from bankrupt Texas after the Civil War and carved an empire out of rawhide and horn. It was said that Chisum had so much land that it would take a man on a good horse all summer to cover it.

New Mexico, where the Murphy-Dolan-Brady ring challenged Chisum's claim and set off the Lincoln County cattle war, which counted among its participants some of the bloodiest pistoleers ever to pull a trigger.

Among them were Jess Evens, George Peppin, Bob Beckwith, Charlie Bowdrie,

Tom O'Folliard, and two friends named Pat Garrett and William Bonney, who ended up on opposite ends of gun barrels. Bonney, better known as Billy the Kid, was a good-humored, jovial lad who had the devil lurking within him. One moment a happy, open-hearted companion, the next he was a blood-splattered psychopath whose own blood was finally splattered by his former friend, Sheriff Pat Garrett. In 1881, when he was twenty-one, Bonney was laid to rest in peace, and the New Mexico Territory has rested more peacefully ever since.

That peace would soon be shattered again as the train from Arizona chugged east into the beclouded sun and toward the Pecos.

Geronimo and his men were crowded onto the floor of the forward car, from which the passenger seats had been removed to make more room. Squatting, the Apaches had slept through the night.

With dawn their eyelids lifted, but not their bodies. Still they sat, shackled, as two soldiers walked through, one carrying a shotgun, the other a rifle. There would be no breakfast — just a noon meal of dried corn and a spartan supper, with a ration of water in between.

178

Geronimo sat against the rumbling wall of the swaying car. He stared straight ahead as the two soldiers strode by. The shotgun soldier spat on the leg of the Apache stretched out next to Geronimo. The Apache didn't move. The two soldiers worked their way back toward the rear door and platform.

Outside the sky turned dark, suddenly foreboding, clouds masking the sun, precursors of the coming rain.

The two soldiers unlocked the door to the second car. It, too, was seatless, loaded with the wounded — one warrior was already dead — and with women and children and the Apache Kid.

The Kid sat, his back braced against the wall, and stared across at the opposite window. The New Mexico countryside raced by. The first driplets of rain streaked the dirty window.

Every mile took the Kid closer to his certain death at the hands of Geronimo and his revenge-sworn Apaches. Every mile took him farther from his birthplace and, most important, from the territory where he knew every canyon, coulee, and rock, the uncharted dominion where he could hide forever. Maybe in time Sieber and Horn could do something, or maybe after a long time Miles and the army would forget about one lone Indian on the loose in a nowhere place. Maybe he would cross into Mexico. But the Apache Kid knew there was no maybe about Geronimo's intentions.

The two soldiers stopped. One nudged the other as they both looked down at a very pregnant young squaw, naked from the waist down, laboring in pain to deliver a baby as a brace of Indian women crouched at her side. The soldiers took in the show for a time, then walked to the rear of the car, unlocked the door, and stepped to the platform and into the light rain.

"Sure does stink in there," said the shotgun soldier.

"Yeah, like old guts," the other soldier said as they opened the door to the caboose.

The sable clouds swirled into a dark cauldron. Lightning ripped across the boiling sky, and rain spilled in sudden torrents against the coursing train as it plunged into a long, black tunnel.

The car was swallowed by darkness. The train whistle screamed. The pregnant squaw screamed, and as the train tore out of the tunnel into the rain again, the baby was born.

The cannonading balled-up figure of the Kid smashed through the window, twisted and tumbled bleeding through the air, slammed on the ground, spun crazily over and over until it seemed his every bone would be broken, then crashed with a shuddering impact against a wet boulder.

Chapter 20

In Globe, Arizona, the bright ball of sun shone out of a yellow sky. Tom Horn had already won the bronc-riding contest, but it appeared that no one would be able to match Charlie Mason's new world record for roping and bulldogging a steer. Mason's time of fifty-one seconds seemed unbeatable.

Cahill and Dawson were betting that Tom Horn could beat it.

Horn was in the saddle waiting to try.

At the judge's signal the wild three-year-old range steer was set loose from a pen and driven at a run by two cowboys toward a marker two hundred fifty yards away. As the red-eyed steer crossed the marker at full speed, the judge fired a second signal, and Horn, riata in hand, spurred after the racing animal.

When he closed to within forty yards, Horn swung the loop of his lariat in a swift, clean circle. At twenty yards he flung the rope like a sling, and its loop settled around the horns of the charging beef and drew tight, tumbling the bewildered animal off its feet as Horn's horse came to an abrupt stop.

Horn flew off his mount, carrying the lash end of the lariat with him, keeping it taut, coiling up the slack while approaching the thrown steer. The crowd stood and yelled as Horn looped a half hitch on the steer's forelegs and another on his hind legs. A third and final knot bunched all four of the stunned animal's legs together in a bouquet of beef.

Done.

"Time," the judge announced, "forty-nine seconds flat! A new world record!"

The rain still pelted into the buckled, unconscious body of the Apache Kid lying at the base of the boulder.

His escape had been discovered when the soldiers returned to the car to disperse the noon meal. The train stopped at Valverde, and telegraph wires tapped out the news north to Santa Fe, south to El Paso, and west back to Bowie. Within hours every fort in both territories had been alerted and patrols were sent out from the Rio San Pedro to the Pecos.

A rain-soaked squad out of Fort Bayard had been reconnoitering for hours, when a scout pointed to the twisted heap that lay in a swale fifty yards from the railroad track.

A trooper reached down, turned the Kid over, and looked into his blood- and rain-streaked face.

"Alive?" the still-mounted sergeant asked, peering out of his slicker.

"Barely."

"Better get him to Bayard," the sergeant said. "What's left of him."

Chapter 21

Al Sieber and Captain Crane walked briskly out of General Miles's headquarters toward a hitching post where Sieber's horse was tied with saddle bags bulging.

"I've never seen the general so flustered," Crane smiled.

"Yeah, he was downright epizootic," said Sieber. He folded a telegram, put it in his breast pocket, and started to mount.

Shana came running toward them. "Mr. Sieber, is it true? Has the Apache Kid escaped?"

"That's part of it," Sieber answered.

"What do you mean?"

"You tell her the other part, Captain." Sieber swung into the saddle. "And don't forget to send that telegraph to Globe." Sieber wheeled his animal around and galloped away through the compound.

"What is it, Captain?" Shana persisted. "What happened?"

"The Kid was badly hurt during the escape. He's been captured again. They're holding him at Fort Bayard." Captain Crane motioned toward the headquarters building. "But that's not what's got General Miles in a flurry. There's something else."

"What, for heaven's sake? Has it got to do with Tom?"

"In a way. I'm sending a telegraph now. Governor Zulick's decided that what the Kid did to Van Zeider constitutes a civilian offense. He telegraphed Miles that the general had no right to put the Kid on that train. Zulick's remanded the Kid to Sieber's custody and authorized him to take the Kid to Tucson, where . . ."

". . . you'll stand trial in a civilian court," a saddle-worn Sieber explained to the Apache Kid in the hospital stockade at Fort Bayard.

The Kid's head was bandaged and covered by his handcuffed hands as he sat listening on a bunk. The Apache Kid lifted his face slowly. It was bruised and discolored.

But that wasn't the only difference. There was a different look in his eyes, a look that had been branded deep. It would be there from now on.

The look was hate.

"We'll get the best lawyer in Tucson," Sieber assured him.

"After Tucson, what?" the Kid whispered.

"We'll have to take it one step at a time."

"Yuma. That'll be the next step. Twenty years in that hellhole in Yuma."

Major Edward McReedy, commanding officer of Fort Bayard, walked down the hallway to where a soldier stood guard. Sieber moved a couple steps toward the major.

"He must be made of catgut," Major McReedy remarked. "We thought he was going to die."

"Maybe part of him did," Sieber replied softly.

"What?"

"Nothing."

"I'll provide you with a wagon and an escort —"

"I don't need any escort."

"I'm sorry, Mr. Sieber. He may be in your custody, but he's my prisoner, and I'm responsible until he's turned over to the proper authorities in Tucson. I'll provide a wagon and escort whenever you're ready to leave."

"Thanks," Sieber grunted.

"You have an idea when that will be?" Major McReedy inquired.

"Whenever the Kid can travel."

"Now." The Kid rose. "I'm ready now."

"Well, I'm not," said Sieber. "I don't travel like a colt no more. I'm plumb tired and saddle sore. We'll leave tomorrow."

Tom Horn, Sergeant Cahill, and Trooper Ward sat at a table in the Globe Café with the scant remnants of three sixteen-ounce steaks and a nearly empty bottle of whiskey in front of them. Someone had thoughtfully provided Horn with a pillow to sit on. A score of customers were eating and drinking at other tables.

"Hey, Sam," Cahill called to the waiter, "fetch another bottle of that tornado juice and give everybody in the house another drink on Sergeant Patrick Cahill, courtesy of Tom Horn, who can rope and ride anything with hair on it!"

Each of the three men had a stack of money in front of him.

Cahill nudged Horn. "Tom, how much prize money did you total out to?"

"Twelve hundred simoleons."

"Hell," said Cahill, "ain't nobody gonna break those records for fifty years — a hundred!"

"We'll do her again next year eh, Tom?" Trooper Ward laughed.

"I might stay right here until then!" Cahill banged a fist into Trooper Ward's shoulder.

The waiter arrived with a fresh quart of whiskey. Cahill handed him the nearly empty bottle. "Here, Sam," Cahill grinned, "give the rest of this to your cat and let him go out and howl at the moon tonight." Cahill laughed and pounded the table, just as a young man entered the café.

"Tom Horn in here?" the young man asked aloud.

"Hell yes," said Cahill. "Right here — the one sitting on the pillow."

"Telegraph, Mr. Horn."

"Thanks." Horn took the telegram and flipped the young man a quarter. He read the message from Crane about the Apache Kid. The young man stood looking at all the money in front of Horn.

"Checked the hotel first," the young man said. "Coulda left the telegraph there. But I made a special trip all the way over here."

"Yeah," said Horn, rising and tossing the young man another quarter. "Thanks."

Horn took his money from the table, stuffed it in his shirt, and started out.

"Hey, Tom," Sergeant Cahill hollered, "where the hell are you going?"

"Fort Bayard," Horn hollered back, and went out the door.

From Fort Bayard the prison wagon creaked past Silver City southwest toward Lordsburg. The wagon was built to hold up to twenty prisoners. This warm and windless day it held only one. The Apache Kid sat on the bench built along the length of the wagon wall and stared out the small barred back window, the only opening in the otherwise completely enclosed lorry.

As he stared he continued to work on the handcuffs. He had been doing just that since the wagon, along with the driver and a mounted guard, with Sieber riding alongside, left Bayard hours ago.

His right hand was compressed, and the Kid kneaded the flesh under the iron bracelet with his left hand. Some of the skin tore away, and the kneading process was now aided by lubricating blood.

Sieber had replaced the Kid's clothes, ripped and shredded by the fall from the broken window, with a pair of booger-red pants and a blue cotton shirt. The Kid still wore his scouting moccasins — and the eagle claw.

Tom Horn had ridden through the night

from Globe. He had left Pilgrim with Sergeant Cahill, bought a good horse, then swapped mounts at the usual posts along the way, Safford, Fort Grant, and Wilcox. Now he was back at Bowie, where he would saddle a fresh horse and head east toward Lordsburg.

Shana saw him ride the burned-out mare across the compound and into the stable. She locked the store and entered the barn as Horn cinched up a strong, deep-chested roan.

"Tom . . ." Shana touched his elbow, and he turned close to her. "You look awful. You've got to get some rest."

"First I've got to meet up with Al and the Kid. I figure that'll be just the other side of Lordsburg."

"A few hours, Tom. What difference will a few hours make?"

"I've got to get there, Shana. But I was coming to see you first."

"Were you?"

"Here." Horn pulled money out of his shirt. "I won twelve hundred in Globe. Keep a thousand for me. Don't want to carry all that much. If we need it in Tucson, I'll come for it. Will you do that?"

"Tom, you need sleep. . . ."

"Will you?"

"Look at you. You're dirty, worn out, half-dead . . . and I think you're wonderful." She reached up and kissed him.

Horn handed her the money, thrust the toe of his boot into the stirrup, legged over the saddle, and went to his spurs.

Sweat and pain streaked down the Kid's contorted face. His right hand was a mass of bloody meat as he worked the iron cuff lower and lower, almost to his bruised knuckles.

The trooper riding alongside Sieber lifted the loosely tied yellow bandana from his neck and wiped at his sweat-mottled face.

"Hotter than hell's hinges," he said, and unscrewed the lid of his canteen. The trooper took a swig, then held the canteen upside-down, showing Sieber that it was empty.

Sieber nodded and pointed down a slope to a stand of trees along a stream about seventy-five yards away. "Give me your canteen. We'll noon here."

"Sounds good." The trooper screwed the lid back on the canteen and handed it to Sieber.

"Tell the driver to pull up. And let the Kid out to stretch his legs and take a leak."

"Yo." The trooper smiled and rode toward the driver as Sieber headed down the slope.

"Pull up, Jess," the trooper instructed the driver. "This'll be our noon stop. Gonna let the Kid out."

Inside, the Apache Kid listened and with a last desperate effort slipped his blood-glossed hand free from the cuff just as the wagon lurched to a stop.

"Come on out, Kid, and do what you haveta." The trooper unlocked and opened the door.

The Apache Kid held his hands together as if they were still shackled and started toward the rear of the lorry.

"This is the last stop before Lordsburg, Kid," the trooper said. "We'll get a hot meal there tonight."

The Kid backed out of the wagon, still concealing his unbound hands. The trooper stretched both arms in the air and twisted his neck to get the trail kinks loose. As the Kid's foot touched the ground near the soldier, he spun and unleashed a left. Fist and handcuff smashed into the trooper's face, felling him.

The Kid sprang toward the downed trooper's nearby horse and pulled the Winchester from its scabbard. Up front the debarking driver, unaware of what had happened, stepped to the ground as a rifle cracked and a bullet crashed into his spine.

The dazed trooper looked up, and as he started to rise, a slug from his own Winchester tore into his forehead.

At the sound of gunfire Sieber dropped the trooper's canteen and turned toward the wagon, reflexively lifting his Colt from its holster. Sieber froze. He saw the Kid holding the Winchester, with the handcuffs dangling from his left wrist.

"Kid!"

A strange look danced into the Apache Kid's eyes. He took quick but careful aim and fired one shot.

The slug shattered Sieber's left shin, tearing apart bone, muscle, and cartilage. The old scout dropped in agony.

A half mile to the west, Tom Horn heard the faint pops of rifle shots and spurred his mount.

The Apache Kid was already riding away on the trooper's horse, holding the reins in his left hand while the blood-wet fingers of his right gripped the Winchester.

Al Sieber half-stumbled, half-crawled back toward the stream. He made it to the water, set down the Colt, and tore away his pant leg. Just above the bootline his leg was a crimson pulp. He dipped his hands into the stream and had just begun to wash the wound, when he heard the hoofbeats. Sieber clawed his Colt and turned back toward the slope.

At the wagon Tom Horn reined in his lathered horse and looked a moment at the two dead men on the ground, then spotted Sieber and galloped down the grade toward the fallen scout.

Horn pulled up just short of Sieber, flew off his mount, and knelt at the wounded man's side.

"Al . . ."

Sieber's lips were thin and white with pain and rage.

"That dirty son of a bitch!" said Al Sieber.

Chapter 22

The prison wagon, with two horses tied behind it, rolled into Fort Bowie. Reins in hand, Horn sat in the driver's seat. Sieber sat next to him, his leg swathed in a blood-soaked makeshift bandage.

Troopers and civilians assembled quickly from all directions and ran alongside, shouting dumb questions that Horn didn't bother to answer and Sieber, nearly unconscious and in shock, couldn't.

"Get the doctor and a stretcher!" Horn hollered as he pulled the wagon up near headquarters. He started to help Sieber, who stirred as the lorry came to a stop. "Lend me a hand here, soldiers!"

The men lifted Sieber off the lorry as General Miles and Captain Crane appeared through the headquarters doorway. Shana came running from the store and the Van Zeider brothers, Emile's arm now in a sling, sauntered over as casually as if they were taking an idle Sunday stroll.

Doctor Jedadiah Barnes and Nurse Thatcher ran past the Van Zeiders in an uncasual hurry. Barnes sized up his patient's condition and barked instructions. "You two lay him on that stretcher. Hatchet, go back and heat up some water — get a move on! Get back, everybody — goddammit, get *back!*" Barnes looked at Horn and pointed to Sieber's leg. "He hit anyplace else?"

"Isn't that enough?" Sieber asked, and lost consciousness.

The troopers carrying Sieber followed Doctor Barnes toward the office-hospital as Barnes was still admonishing them to "get a move on."

"Are you all right, Tom?" Shana touched his arm.

"Yeah." Horn nodded, then turned toward Miles and Crane. "There's two dead troopers in the wagon."

Four soldiers moved toward the rear of the prison wagon, untied the two horses, and opened the unlocked door.

"And where," General Nelson Appleton Miles spat out, "is the Apache Kid?"

The Apache Kid leaned over the carcass of the horse he had ridden to death. He lifted the trooper's Winchester out of its boot, uncinched the saddle and pulled it free from the dead animal. He let the saddle fall on the ground but picked up the saddle blanket, worked it into a roll, and shoved it under his armpit, pressing it against his body. He did all this without haste or concern. He knew there was no other living human being, white or red, within twenty miles of this stillborn spot. For now no one could harm him, manacle him, pen him. No one could touch or see him.

Carrying the rolled blanket under his left arm, from which the handcuffs still dangled, and with the Winchester cold against the palm of his right hand, he stepped over the legs of the dead horse.

The Apache Kid was walking to where the sun had set, heading home along the Dragoon Mountains.

Al Sieber lay conscious now in a bed at the infirmary. Horn, Shana, Doctor Barnes, and Nurse Thatcher were still there. Barnes and Thatcher had washed out the wound, made what repairs were possible, set splints on the leg, and wrapped it tight.

"I'm gonna track him down," said Sieber, "and I'm gonna kill him."

"Not tonight you ain't," Doctor Barnes advised. "Tonight you're gonna get some rest. You lost a bucket of blood. Hatchet, see if you can blow out that lamp without knocking it over."

"Tom," said Sieber, "I want you to —"

"Not now, Al," Horn interrupted. "You do what Jedadiah says. We'll talk about it tomorrow."

Sieber nodded reluctantly, then breathed deeply as Nurse Thatcher blew out the lamp.

"I'll be nearby," the nurse said. "If you need anything just call out."

Sieber closed his eyes, and the others left the room.

"Hatchet, you go home. I'll sleep on the cot tonight," Doctor Barnes said as they entered the waiting room. "No sense in both of us hanging around."

"Why don't *you* go home?" Thatcher replied. "Maybe you'll even put on a fresh shirt tomorrow — that one's getting rusty."

"Go home you old spigot. I'm the head limb skinner around here — and this shirt's good for another week."

"Good night, you two," Nurse Thatcher said to Shana and Horn as she walked to the door.

"Tom . . ." Doctor Barnes spoke almost in a whisper so Sieber couldn't hear even if he were awake. "This isn't the time to tell him, but I might as well tell you."

"That bad?" Horn thumbed his chin.

"Not for an ordinary man. But Sieber's not an ordinary man. His scouting days are all behind him."

"That's a hard dose. You sure?"

"The only thing he'll ride from now on is a pair of crutches."

"Damn!" Horn whispered.

"You look like you took a flogging yourself, boy," Barnes said. "Go home and get some bed rest."

Horn nodded. He and Shana walked toward the door.

"Good night, Doctor." Shana managed a smile.

"Good night," Doctor Jedadiah Barnes said. "And let me tell you something, young lady. You're the prettiest female either side of the Pecos, just in case somebody hasn't already told you."

The scent of early-summer flowers drifted up and through Fort Bowie from the dark fields below.

"Tom," said Shana as she unlocked the door, "would you like to come in? I'll fix you something to eat."

"Thanks, Shana. Don't feel like eating."

"A shot of hooty owl?"

"That neither."

"Oh, Tom, I'm so sorry. I know how close the three of you were."

"Do you? If I had just got there a little earlier, everything would've been different. If . . ." Horn shrugged. "But that's a mountain of an if."

"You can't blame yourself. You and Mr. Sieber were doing everything you could to help him."

"I guess so."

"Then *why?* Why did he do it?"

" 'Cause it was the Kid who'd have to do time in Yuma."

"That didn't give him reason to —"

"No, it didn't. But we haven't used much reason in dealing with the Apaches either."

"You can't condone what the Kid's done?"

"No, I can't *condone* it. But the Kid got into this because he threw a knife into a white man who was trying to kill me. And I can't forget that . . ." Horn turned and started to walk away. ". . . and a lot of other things. Good night, Shana."

A silent silhouette moved in the darkness along the riverbank through the dejected cottonwoods toward the mesquite and cactus that led to the slumbering San

201

Carlos Reservation. The Apache Kid had tied the dangling bracelet to his wrist to prevent any rattle that would betray his presence. He still carried the Winchester.

The Apache Kid noiselessly pulled aside a skin covering the entrance of the wickiup and peered into the dark interior. What he looked for was not here. A thin, aged Indian was sleeping between two squaws, both of them old and fat.

At the third wickiup the Kid found what he had come for. A young squaw slept in the arms of her husband. A thin nightshirt lay loosely on her well-proportioned body. The Kid stepped into the warm, dark privacy of the hut. He raised the Winchester and brought the butt of the rifle down hard on the skull of the sleeping brave.

The young squaw bolted up. At the sight of her stricken husband, she started to scream, but the Apache Kid's fist slammed into the side of her face, and she fell back unconscious.

The Kid lifted the young squaw over his shoulder, picked up his Winchester, and walked with his prize out of the wickiup into the black of the simmering night.

Chapter 23

The bugler blew assembly. Fort Bowie was already bustling with activity. Besides the troopers gathering into formation and the civilians going about their early-morning business, a delegation of reservation Indians milled near General Miles, who stood watching from the porch of his headquarters. Tom Horn approached the general. Miles ignored the former scout's presence.

"Where they going, General?" Horn inquired.

"The Apache Kid's crimes are no longer a civilian matter. I'm ordering Captain Crane to bring him in."

"That's a tall order," said Horn, walking away.

Captain Crane was ready to mount as Tom Horn appeared.

"Morning, Captain," Horn greeted.

"You heard what happened last night?" Crane asked.

"No."

"The Kid visited one of the villages at San Carlos. Killed an Indian and kidnapped his wife."

Horn did his best not to react visibly to the captain's news. Crane mounted.

"You'll never find him, Captain."

"We could if you came along." Crane stared at Horn for a moment. Without answer Horn turned and moved off.

He saw Shana coming out of the store carrying a tray filled with food and a pot of coffee.

"Good morning, Tom."

"Morning."

"I thought I'd take some breakfast over to Mr. Sieber. Care to come along?"

"I would." Horn reached out and took the tray.

When Horn and Shana entered, Doctor Jedadiah Barnes and Nurse Thatcher were in the dialectic throes of discussing a clean shirt she held in her hand.

"*You* wear the damn thing, Hatchet. I'm not taking this shirt off until it's dirty, and it's damn well as clean as it was the day I put it on. Good morning, Shana. Hello, Tom."

"I bring this old curmudgeon a fresh shirt," exclaimed Nurse Thatcher in disgust, "and he's too damn stubborn to put it on!"

"I'll put it on next week. Go back to your bedpans and leave us in peace."

"I think I'm going to quit."

"You been promising that for ten years."

"I've been waiting for you to get some-body else." Nurse Thatcher turned again to Shana and Horn and added, "But no-body with the sense of a cockroach would put up with him."

"What you got there?" Doctor Barnes pointed to the tray in Tom's hand.

"Shana made some breakfast for Al. Is it all right if we go in?"

"Move on in," said Doctor Barnes.

Al Sieber was sitting up in bed looking out the window when Shana and Horn en-tered.

"See you're up already," said Horn, set-ting the tray on a table next to the bed.

"Hell, no, I ain't *up*. But I'm awake. Who can sleep with all these damn bugles blowing!" Sieber pointed to the tray. "That for me?"

"Shana fixed it." Horn nodded.

"Didn't figure *you* did. Looks too orga-nized. Morning, Miss Ryan."

"Good morning." Shana smiled and lifted the large blue-and-white-checked napkin from the tray, revealing a plate with eight strips of bacon, four scrambled eggs, three slices of toast, and jam next to the coffeepot.

"Hell," said Sieber, "the king of England don't eat any better than that."

"The king of England's name is Victoria," Horn observed, "and she's the queen."

"Never mind the details; just pour the coffee," ordered Sieber.

From outside there came another order, and the troopers moved out behind Captain Crane.

"What's going on out there?" asked Sieber after taking a healthy gulp of coffee.

"Our Captain Crane and half the troopers at Fort Bowie are going after the Kid."

"Fat chance." Sieber dug into the breakfast.

"Yep," Horn answered.

"These eggs musta been layed by some prize hen, ma'am. Never tasted 'em this good before."

"Thank you."

"Tom. Ain't you going?" Sieber asked.

"Going where?"

"You know damn well. After the Kid."

"Haven't been asked to go."

Horn and Shana visited with Sieber until he finished eating, then went back to her apartment behind the store, where Shana duplicated the breakfast for Horn. It was Tom's first hot food since the steak in Globe.

Afterward, as Tom carried his fourth cup of coffee with him, Shana officially opened the store for business. Then she remembered something. "Tom, I have your money in the safe. Shall I get it for you?"

"We won't be needing it for the Kid's trial," said Horn. "There's no lawyer in the world could get him off now. Might as well leave it there till I figure out what I'm going to do."

"Do you have any ideas?"

"Well, I've got two hundred to go with that thousand. Might buy out a claim — or even a ranch."

"If you're considering going into business, I have a proposition to make you."

"I'd like to listen," he smiled, and sipped from the coffee mug.

"The Van Zeiders have offered me three thousand dollars for the franchise. The store's too much for me, but I could use a partner. Would you consider buying half interest for a thousand dollars?"

"No." Horn paused as disappointment settled on Shana's face. "But I would consider buying a third interest for a thousand."

As Shana smiled and stepped toward him, the brothers Van Zeider entered the store. "Good morning!" Karl beamed. "Well, Mr. Horn, I'm surprised you aren't leading the expedition."

"I am. Didn't you see me riding out there in front?"

"Tom has other plans," Shana said. "He's become my partner in the store."

The brothers Van Zeider exchanged glances; then Karl fingered the gold fob. "Oh, I see." Karl Van Zeider nodded. "Then I suppose it's too late to make you another offer?"

"Yes," Shana replied, looking at Horn.

"Well come along Emile. We have work to do." Van Zeider led his brother toward the door. When they were nearly there, he turned and added as an afterthought, "By the way, congratulations, Mr. Horn. I'd say this setup beats . . ." He looked at Shana. ". . . living with the Apaches." Both Van Zeiders smiled and walked out.

Horn started after them, but Shana stopped him. She took the mug from his fist. "Let me get you some more coffee" — she extended her right hand — "partner."

Horn put his big hand around hers.

"Thanks, partner."

Outside, Karl and Emile Van Zeider

walked toward the *cantina* in silence for some distance. Emile adjusted the sling on his arm. "A hell of a lot of good it did," he said, "to get rid of Ryan."

"Shut up!" Karl snapped.

Chapter 24

The sun came up a bold red ball over the rim of the eastern ridge. The Apache Kid grabbed the sleeping young squaw by her wrist and pulled her toward him. For a merciful moment she had forgotten where she was. But the cruel realization seared like a hot brand in her brain, and she remembered. She would remember the last two days and nights as long as she lived.

The Apache Kid had satisfied his lust time after time. Now he would take her again, high on the rocky cove where they had spent the night. He pulled off her torn garment and moved himself onto her trembling body. He pressed his mouth against her bruised face and onto her lips. She felt his bone-hard hands, with the iron cuffs still around one wrist, prowling over the flesh of her naked body. She closed her eyes and prepared for what would come. She didn't know whether her husband was alive or dead, but she wished that she were dead.

She knew she wasn't. The Apache Kid reminded her again that she was still alive

— alive enough to feel pain and humiliation and hate.

For four days and nights Captain Crane and his command combed the Superstition Mountains, searching for tracks or signs. There weren't any — or if there were, none of the troopers was capable of reading them. Without the scouts they saw only empty ridges, vacant ravines, desolate coulees, and naked peaks.

As they climbed higher they dismounted and led their animals across razorback rocks. This was not horse country. Only goats and mountain sheep could find footing, not troopers whose boots were made for stirrups instead of steep, towering terrain.

The Apache Kid and his captive were nowhere near the area the troopers searched. They had left the Superstitions and moved along a stream that snaked south and led to a valley where cattle grazed. The Kid knew if there were cattle, there would be a ranch.

On a Sunday morning the ranch lay peaceful, compatible with the tree-lined stream — a house, a barn, a corral with a dozen horses, a pen with as many pigs, and an overcrowded chicken coop.

With the young squaw kneeling at his side, the Apache Kid watched from distant cover as the family, Sunday clean from their Saturday baths and dressed in their churchgoing best, walked from the house toward the buckboard. A tall, angular man who looked more like a preacher than a rancher was followed by his pregnant wife and three small children of assorted ages and sizes.

The Kid waited while the buckboard pulled away from the house and disappeared to the south; then he looked down at the squaw. She was a pathetic sight. Even though she had washed in the refreshing stream the evening before, she was now worn and weary from the ordeal she had endured through the night and morning at the Kid's hands. The remnants of the thin nightshirt hung ripped and loose, exposing most of her abused body.

The Kid pulled her up and shoved her toward the ranch. He walked alongside, with the Winchester in his right hand and the handcuff suspended from the left.

The Kid paused in front of the corral. He looked over the horses. The Appaloosa gelding wasn't the biggest of the herd, but the Kid liked the look of the animal, broad of chest and with finely muscled legs. That was the one he would take when he finished the business at hand. He shoved the squaw into the barn.

The Kid found what he was looking for. He handed the squaw a hammer and chisel, put his left hand on the anvil, and stretched the loose cuff taut with his right. The Winchester leaned against a stack of hay, within easy reach.

The squaw struck at the lip of the Kid's cuff. He felt pain but didn't wince. He nodded at the squaw, and she struck again and again.

A sleepy-eyed, toothless man, wearing trousers, slippers, and a nightshirt but carrying a handgun with cartridge belt and holster, came out of the house, cocked his head, and listened to the sound of the hammering. Then he moved toward the barn.

One, two more blows, and the handcuffs snapped loose just at the instant the toothless man appeared at the door with his gun pointed at the Kid.

"What the hell do you think you're doing?" the man blustered. For answer the Apache Kid in a swift motion grabbed up the rifle, shoved the squaw in front of him, and fired past her, hitting the toothless man in the chest.

But the man's gun went off as he fell, and a bullet tore into the girl's side. She staggered but stayed on her feet.

The Kid walked to where the man had fallen. His foot went under the man's shoulder, and with Winchester still pointed, the Kid rolled him face up.

The toothless man gazed with open but unseeing eyes. The Kid lifted the gun and cartridge belt from the ground, motioned at the wounded squaw to follow, then walked toward the Appaloosa.

A set of broken handcuffs lay on top of General Nelson Appleton Miles's neat and orderly desk. The general puffed a cigar as the tall, angular man went on with his story.

". . . When we got back from church we found Jess. That's — that was — our hired hand — shot dead in the barn. Two of my best horses gone, a knife, some airtights, and —"

"Airtights?"

"Canned goods, General."

"Your hired hand wasn't a churchgoer?"

"No sir, but a good man. Oh, there was some other blood in the barn."

"Let's hope it was the Apache Kid's.

Come in," Miles responded to the knock on the office door. An adjutant entered. "What is it, Pitt?"

"You wanted to be notified when Captain Crane came in, sir. Well, he's coming in now."

"Thank you."

"And those Indians from the reservation are still waiting."

"Yes." Miles rose and picked up his hat from the hanger. "Well come along. We may have some good news, Mr. . . . Bell-camp, is it?"

"Bellknap," answered the tall, angular man.

"Yes, Bellknap." Miles adjusted his hat more to his liking, took the handcuffs from his desk, and led the way. "Come along."

Al Sieber sat on a chair on the Ryan store's porch — his leg, still in splints, resting on a box — and watched as Crane's contingent led their bone-weary animals, some of which were limping. So were some of the soldiers. Tom Horn walked out of the store and stood a moment next to the pair of crutches tilted against the wall beside Sieber.

"Well," Sieber spat out a spray of tobacco juice, "at least he got back."

"Yeah. I'll go over and see what else he got . . . or didn't."

"He didn't." Sieber spat again.

Nine reservation Indians waited in front of the headquarters building as Miles, Bellknap, and Pitt came out. Miles approached Crane. The captain and his men stood sore and gritty from the expedition. In contrast, General Miles was fresh and immaculate and most military.

"Did you find the Apache Kid, Captain?"

"Not a trace of him, sir."

"Well, *here's* a trace of him, Captain." Miles brought up the broken cuffs he had held behind his back and thrust them close to the Captain's dirty, stubbled face. "Why did you come back before you completed your mission?"

"Horses went lame, sir, and some of the men —"

"Then tomorrow you'll take fresh horses and fresh troopers, go out again, and carry out your mission."

"Yes, sir."

"By the way" — Miles pointed to the reservation Apaches — "those Indians, they're relatives of the girl who was stolen. They've volunteered to help find the Apache Kid. See if they can be of some use."

"Yes, sir."

"But find the Apache Kid — dead or alive, find the Apache Kid and bring him in!"

Miles turned smartly and marched back into his headquarters as Horn walked up to Crane.

"Well," said Horn, "your 'headquarters general' is finally showing a little sense."

"Using Indians to chase an Indian."

Horn walked back to the store and stood next to Sieber.

"When they going after him again?" the old scout asked.

"Tomorrow."

"I hope they don't find him. You know why?"

"Yeah, I know why." Horn started into the store. "They won't," he added.

The Apache Kid, with the white-hot blade of the knife in his hand, knelt over the wounded, nearly naked squaw, who lay by the campfire. Her eyes burned with fear and pain, and as the Kid pressed the scorching blade against her bleeding flesh, cauterizing the wound, she passed out.

Chapter 25

It was almost dark as Karl Van Zeider walked into the stable of the Van Zeider Brothers Livery. A loaded wagon was covered with heavy tarp. Emile Van Zeider and Pete Curtain each sat on a bale of hay, a bottle of whiskey on a stool between them. The sling had been removed from his arm, and Emile puffed on a cigar as he drank.

"Goods all loaded?" Karl Van Zeider asked.

Emile exhaled and nodded toward the wagon.

"Did you take the labels off?"

Emile nodded again.

"All right, then." Van Zeider fingered the fob. "Hitch up and leave before dawn. With luck you'll be in Nogales Saturday."

Emile looked up at his brother. They were a study in contrasts, the Van Zeiders, the result of different mothers. Karl was tall, slim, and smooth. Educated, assured, and cunning, he was a cold creature but civil, always civil and controlled. Karl a man of moderation where liquor, women, and tobacco were concerned but immoderate in the ambition department. Emile was bigger and coarse, with a hogshead face, pocked and with piggish eyes. He was a man who took orders along with whiskey, women, and cigars and whose ambition was only for more of the same — much more.

"You don't mind," Emile smiled, "if me and Pete spend the weekend in Nogales, do you?"

"With all that money? Yes, I do mind. And tell señor Delegado that the price has gone up to fifty dollars a case."

"What if he won't pay?"

"He'll pay." Van Zeider started to walk away.

Emile inhaled the smoke of his cigar. "Karl, I was just thinking — our old friend Geronimo is long since in Florida by now."

"So?"

"So," shrugged Emile, "I kinda miss him, that's all. He sure brought things to a boil around here. Looks like the Apache Kid's aiming to take his place."

"Geronimo can be in hell as far as I'm concerned. He's no longer of any use and as for the Apache Kid, he's just one lone, stupid savage who won't bring in enough troopers to line our pockets. We've got to look to other sources. The Apache Kid amounts to an insignificant, impertinent pest."

"Tell that to the cavalry."

"Never mind the cavalry. I'm just telling you — get to Nogales and back as soon as you can; we've got business to take care of." Karl Van Zeider walked out of the stable into the darkness.

Pete Curtain shrugged. "Well, you tried."

"Who knows, Pete?" Emile swallowed a shot of whiskey. "Maybe we'll have some trouble with the wagon, have to lay over in Nogales a day or two anyhow." Emile worked his wounded shoulder around. It felt pretty good.

Al Sieber watched from his chair on the store porch as Karl Van Zeider walked by without greeting. Sieber spat tobacco and glanced inside at Horn and Shana.

She held a clipboard and pencil, making notations. There was a look of comfort and satisfaction on her face as she watched Tom Horn move to the next shelf.

"Look here, Shana," he said. "I don't see any sense in this inventory business. It'll just be different tomorrow."

"But this is part of storekeeping," she smiled.

"Well, it's the part I don't like." He moved a step closer. "Matter of fact, the only part I do like is —" Horn stopped as he saw Sieber outside rise with difficulty and reach for his crutches. "Hey, Al, where you going?"

Sieber wedged the crutch handles under his armpits and started to move.

"Al . . ." Horn moved to the open door. "I asked you where —"

"I heard you," Sieber snorted. "No law against a man getting a drink around here, is there?"

"Well, just hold on a minute," Horn smiled, "and I'll get a drink with you."

"You tend to your beans and bacon!" Sieber snapped, and started to hobble away.

"Okay, Al," Horn said with a wounded tone. "I'll see you later."

"Suit yourself," Sieber shot back from the night.

Tom Horn walked into the store, closed the door, and looked down at the floor. He thought of the countless days and nights Sieber and he had shared without a floor beneath them, with only grass or sand or rock. Their home had been anywhere they unsaddled their horses. He thought of the days when Sibi's Boys rode to hell with their hair on fire and came back to laugh about it.

Shana broke the long silence. "I thought we might offer him a job here at the store, but . . ."

"Shana, he's only got one thing on his mind."

"What'll happen when he finds out he won't ever be able to go after the Kid?"

"I don't know. I flat out don't know. But it's better that he can't. I think the Kid'd kill anything or anybody who tried to take him."

"Tom," she moved close. "I'm glad you're not going after him. No matter what he's done."

"Maybe I'm afraid to go."

"I don't believe that." She put her arms around his waist as if to protect him and herself.

"Good sense to be afraid of some things. They say an Apache only knows two emotions — fear and hate."

"I don't believe that." Her arms still encircled him.

"Neither do I," he smiled. "I've seen different."

"How long," Shana withdrew her arms, "did you live with the Apaches?"

"Almost three years on and off. It was

Al's idea. Wanted me to get to know the Apache language and their ways. Said it would make me a better scout."

"I think it made you a better person."

"Don't know about that" — Horn shook his head — "but I got to like it."

Shana walked a few steps toward the counter, then turned and faced him again. She wondered if it was proper, if she had the right to ask the question.

Horn read the struggle in her face. "What is it, Shana? What's wrong?"

"When you say you lived with them . . . does that mean you . . ."

"It means I lived with them."

"You found the Apache . . . women . . . attractive?"

"Some of them — and attentive."

"Was there one particularly attractive — and attentive?" A strange sound had come into her voice, a sound unlike her, a sound she didn't savor. "I'm sorry, Tom. It was crass of me to ask."

"I'll tell you this," Horn said, moving to her. "There was no one like you."

"At least you managed to say goodbye to all that," she smiled, and blew out the lamp on the counter.

"No." The store was now illuminated by a solitary lamp on the wall. Horn moved with his easy, pantherine grace and blew out the flame. "There's no word for hello or goodbye in Apache. Man just comes and goes." He moved close enough to touch her, but didn't.

"That is strange," she whispered in the darkness.

"They're afraid if you make some farewell gesture you might die and never come back." As he spoke her face was inching nearer and nearer, until she kissed him as he finished.

It was more than a kiss, and both of them knew it. It was an invitation, a prelude, a consent. It wasn't only their lips that met and melded. Their bodies molded into each other — his, lean and strong and hard, pressing; hers, soft and pliant, receiving.

Civilization was a million miles from here; Boston, another time, another world. Laws and rules and customs were stripped away. This was the West, still a wilderness, savage and naked but truthful. She knew the truth. She felt it coursing through her.

"I'm glad," she said, trembling, "you're not going away."

He lifted her from the ground, one arm around her back, the other under the bend of her legs.

"Tonight I'll be your squaw," she whispered in the dark.

"Tonight," he said, "you'll be my woman," and carried her to the apartment.

Chapter 26

Against the dawning sun the Appaloosa picked its way carefully along the ragged ridges of the high country and negotiated the narrow, hazardous defile. The Apache Kid now wore the gun and belt of the hired man he had killed. Behind him the mare carrying the dazed and wounded Indian woman followed, trying to duplicate the Appaloosa's footing.

The squaw was barely conscious, her hand pressing against her side at her wound, which had opened. Blood spilled between her fingers down her naked leg. She breathed in labored spurts, fighting for strength to go on. Then she no longer fought or cared. She could endure no more, nor did she want to. She wanted to be free. But there was only one freedom. It was not on this earth. Suddenly she felt light, exalted, euphoric. She dropped the reins. She knew the end had come — another beginning.

She tumbled from the horse and plummeted below, slamming crazily, bouncing, twisting, crashing over and over against the jagged rocks.

The Kid looked back for a moment at the riderless horse and then below.

His expression never changed.

Two of the reservation Indians stayed with Crane and the main contingent. The others forked out trying to pick up the Kid's tracks.

It was past noon when one of the Apaches who had left Crane motioned to his companion and pointed toward a squadron of buzzards circling far in the distance.

One of the Indians waited at the site near the buzzards; the other rode back for Crane. Neither had been given a weapon. General Miles didn't believe in arming Apaches under any circumstances.

When Crane arrived, the waiting Indian pointed below toward the buzzards at work on the flesh of the young squaw. Crane pulled his rifle from its boot and fired. The dirty black birds screamed, and feathers flecked off as they flew away.

The Apache Kid studied the tracks without dismounting. Even on horseback he could read all he needed to know: A four-up wagon with a heavy load had passed, heading southwest toward Sonora,

227

not more than an hour ago. He reined the Appaloosa, dug his moccasins into the animal's flanks, and rode directly south.

The four tired horses pulling the heavy, rattling wagon labored against the incline on the trail that wound south to Sonora. Pete Curtain snapped the reins, ribboned through his thick fingers and the horses hastened their pace. Emile Van Zeider took the first puff from a fresh cigar and passed a whiskey bottle to Curtain, who took a pull and passed it back.

"By this time tomorrow," Van Zeider remarked, "we'll be in Nogales."

It was his last remark.

A bullet through his head put a finish to all his remarks.

Pete Curtain reflexively turned toward the stricken man. Even before Van Zeider's cigar and whiskey bottle hit the boot of the wagon, the second and third bullets tore into the driver's chest, and Curtain let loose of the ribbons as he fell dead from the seat.

The Apache Kid watched for a moment from behind the wind-rubbed boulder at the crest of the incline, then walked to the Appaloosa, mounted with Winchester still in hand, and rode toward the waiting wagon.

The Kid looked at the dead face of Emile Van Zeider. Van Zeider with his shotgun had triggered the Kid's troubles. His end had come too swiftly, too easily. The Kid thought to himself that he should have made Van Zeider suffer. He thought of taking Apache vengeance on the dead body. Instead, he went through the pockets of the corpses, kept what he wanted, then jumped aboard the wagon and ripped the tarp with his knife.

A few minutes later the Apache Kid rode south on the Appaloosa, and drank from a whiskey bottle. He had unhitched the four horses, and the wagon now burned behind him. The fire intensified until the volatile fluid within the bottles began a series of explosions and set off a blaze of flame and smoke that could be seen miles away.

Chapter 27

"General Miles," Karl Van Zeider fumed, "I demand the immediate apprehension of this barbarian."

"You do!" Miles remarked from behind his desk.

"Yes, I do. It seems inconceivable to me that the whole United States Army — horses, foot and dragoons — can't catch one half-naked Apache."

"It does to me, too," Miles replied.

"I have influence in high places, General, both civilian and military, you can be sure —"

"I can be sure of one thing, Mr. Van Zeider — if you're about to threaten me, *don't*. I've faced bigger odds and prevailed. I never went to West Point, but I have a Congressional Medal of Honor that damn few West Pointers ever won. I've dealt with military snobbery and congressional bungling. I've dealt with the Nez Percé and the Sioux, and by the Lord Harry I'll deal with the Apache Kid without any intimidation from you!"

"I want to see him hanged," said Van Zeider.

"So do I, Mr. Van Zeider. So do we all. Captain Crane —"

"Captain Crane doesn't know a rock from a toad."

"That's enough of *that!* Captain Crane will —" A knock on the door interrupted General Miles. "Come in."

The adjutant entered. "Tom Horn's here."

"Tell him to come in." Miles turned to Van Zeider. "I've sent for the man who knows every rock and toad in the territory. Come in, Mr. Horn. Sit down."

"I'll stand," said Horn without greeting either man.

"You heard what happened to Mr. Van Zeider's brother?"

"He got caught smuggling whiskey across the border," Horn replied.

Van Zeider took a step. "Look here you —"

"Take it easy, Van Zeider," Horn said without looking at him. "Yeah, I heard," Horn answered Miles.

"And about the Indian girl?"

"That, too."

"I've talked to Mr. Sieber." Miles lapsed into diplomacy, "Unfortunately, his injury, which you well know was inflicted by the Apache Kid, prevents him from going after this cold-blooded murderer. Mr. Horn, I'm giving you that assignment — at full pay, of course. Captain Crane —"

"Now hold up, General. In the first place, you're the one who said that scouts were obsolete."

"I was wrong," Miles admitted — "at least in this case."

"Well, I took you at your word, because in the second place, General, you're not talking to a scout; you're talking to a store-keeper. I'm a storekeeper."

"And the Apache Kid is a murderer!"

"I don't deny that. There's a lot of murderers on the loose."

"I can't force you to do it," Miles reasoned, "but —"

"No, you can't."

". . . but I can ask you," Miles's voice became oratorical, "on behalf of every decent citizen of this territory —"

"Save the speeches; I'm not listening." Horn pointed to the wall behind Miles's desk. "Why don't you pick up your gold sword and go chase him yourself?"

Horn turned and started to walk away. Karl Van Zeider blocked his path. "You're a filthy coward!"

"Get out of the way." Horn shoved him hard, smashing Van Zeider against the wall, then walked out.

Captain Crane stood outside the headquarters building. He started to say something as Tom Horn walked by, but Horn paid no heed and kept walking.

Horn brushed by a customer just leaving the store and entered. Shana was at the cash register, and Al Sieber stood propped by his pair of crutches near the counter.

"Well?" Sieber demanded.

"Well, what?" Horn was close to trembling.

"Now you been asked. What did you tell him?"

"Al," Horn pleaded, "don't ask me."

"I *am* asking you." Sieber took a step on the crutches. "I raised him from a pup. But when your pup turns out to be a mad dog, it's your job to kill him. Well, I ain't able to do that, Tom. I know I'll be a cripple for the rest of my life. But I raised you, too — and I'm asking you."

"Somebody else'll get him."

"Not before he spills blood on every road and ditch in the territory. Never mind what he's done to me. He'll go on killing and plundering until he's shot down like the mad dog he's turned into. Now what about it!"

Horn said nothing. He lowered his look

from the old scout's stare. But Sieber knew the answer. He dropped his right crutch and smashed his big fist into Horn's face, knocking him into a row of flour sacks. Sieber himself nearly fell with the blow.

Horn did not wipe the blood from his mouth. Nor did he look up at the man who struck him.

Al Sieber struggled and finally managed to pick up the fallen crutch. "Move your things outta my place," Sieber said, hobbling toward the door, "and stay the hell away from me. I haven't got any sons anymore."

When Sieber left, Shana rushed to Horn, but he waved her away and rose to his feet.

"He'll get over it, Tom," she tried to reassure him. "He'll understand."

"No he won't," said Horn, "because he's right. But I just can't do it. The Kid'll never let anyone bring him in. If I found him I couldn't shoot him from behind." Horn tasted the warm, sweet blood at his mouth, then wiped it clean.

Tom Horn rented a room in one of the boardinghouses and continued to work at the store. In three months, the reward for the Apache Kid, dead or alive, escalated in direct proportion to his depredations, from one thousand to six thousand dollars.

A second and third young squaw were kidnapped, ravaged, and left dead. Reservation Indians along with Crane and every available trooper pursued the phantom killer who roamed unseen — except by some of his victims — under the sizzling-hot summer sun and the cold rays of the inconstant moon. The Apache Kid pillaged from as far north as Socorro, south past the border into Chihuahua and Sonora — from mountains and buttes through dry riverbeds, ranches, and deserts. Another of Van Zeider's freight wagons was ambushed, the driver and guard killed, and the wagon set aflame. General Miles even armed some of the Indian guards at the reservation. Two of them were killed and their ammunition stolen.

By summer's end the United States Army was no closer to catching the Apache Kid than it had ever been. Time and again the Kid watched invisible from a vantage point as sweat-soaked patrols passed in the distance, seeking tracks or signs and finding only failure and frustration. The men of these patrols were the same troopers with whom the Kid, along with Sieber and Horn, had once ridden.

The Kid knew that Al Sieber was no longer capable of riding with the cavalry, but he strained for the sight of Tom Horn and was relieved and pleased that he never saw him.

The people at Fort Bowie, civilian and military, were not pleased by the sight of Tom Horn. They never said it to his face, but they whispered of everything from apathy to cowardice to complicity.

Horn and Sieber hadn't spoken since the blow was struck. Whenever they met, Sieber looked straight ahead. Horn would slow down and hope the old scout might give a sign or word to change things, but Sieber hobbled on as if Horn didn't exist.

Shana asked Tom if she could talk to Sieber, but Horn told her that nothing Shana could say or do would sway the old scout's attitude. Things would just have to stay as they were until something happened. And things stayed as they were between Horn and Shana. There were embraces and good-night kisses, but after that single night of complete intimacy and consummated passion, he never again ventured into her bedroom.

For Shana Ryan it had been a delirious, dizzying, explosive experience alternating between initial exotic plunging pain and soaring serene rapture, from sublime sub-mission to joint participation to eager, rav-ening initiative. Horn was sensual yet savage, gentle, and aggressive. She didn't want to think of it, but it was as if she hadn't lost herself to one man that night — it was as if she had been made love to by half a dozen. She often lay in that same bed reliving everything she could re-member, thinking of the only man she'd ever been with and somehow a little afraid to be with him again. They never spoke of that night, but sometimes even when cus-tomers were present in midday or while they were having dinner or walking along the compound, a look would come be-tween them, and each knew the other was remembering that night.

That look came between them now, late at night in the store, as they finished the monthly inventory. Shana purposely broke the spell.

"Well, that's it." She put the clipboard and pencil on the counter. "I didn't re-alize —"

"That's it, all right," Horn interrupted. "Business is about half what it used to be."

"That's part of storekeeping too," she smiled, "good times and bad."

"Come on, Shana — you know people

are staying away from here as much as they can on account of me."

"That's not true."

"The hell it's not. They look at me as if *I* was the Apache Kid." He gazed out the window. "Maybe it's best if I leave Bowie."

Shana walked to him, turned him toward her, and kissed him. It was not a kiss of passion, but more of comfort and assurance. "Best for whom? Not for you and me. I'm not a squaw, Tom Horn, that you can just walk away from. Am I?"

"No." He held her. "It wouldn't be easy to walk away from you."

They kissed again, not a kiss of comfort and assurance but a kiss that stirred the memory of their night.

"Tom, the night that I was your squaw . . ."

"No, Shana, you weren't. Don't say that. It wasn't that way, not with you . . . not with you." Both his hands touched her face. "I'd . . . better get out of here."

He picked up his hat and went for the door.

"Tom, tomorrow's Sunday. Let's go on a picnic, just you and I. I'll fix a basket. Would you like to do that?"

"I would," he said, and went out the door.

He walked along the moonlit grounds

and turned a corner. A fist crashed into his face. Four burly men began to beat him. They were shadows but struck with substance. Horn struck back. One went down, then another.

A knife glinted and slashed across Horn's shoulder. Horn hit the knifer, who spun into a window, shattering it.

Two sentries ran toward the noise.

At the sight of the sentries the attackers scattered, absorbed by the chocolate shadows. Karl Van Zeider had been watching from a corner. He retreated and disappeared in the darkness.

"Horn," one of the sentries asked, "is that you?"

"Yeah."

"You all right?" the other inquired.

"I'm all right."

"That's too bad," came an answer.

Tom Horn rubbed at the blood on his shoulder, picked up his hat, and walked toward the place where he slept.

Chapter 28

It was almost noon.

Tom Horn lay on the blanket beside the clean stream that sparkled in the radiant summer sun, his hat near the nearly empty picnic basket and his gunbelt unfastened and laid in a loop by his side. Shana sat watching him. Even in these pleasant, peaceful surroundings, he didn't seem completely relaxed. There was always the edge of readiness about him. She noticed that the butt of the pistol, as always, was close to his hand.

"Tom, would you like some more chicken?"

"No, thanks. But that was the best bird I ever did taste."

"Thank you. A little more wine?"

"No, thanks. Can't remember the last time I had wine. Sure went down smooth, but it hasn't got much of a bolt to it."

"It's not supposed to," Shana smiled. "It's a social drink."

"By that you mean civilized?"

"That," she said, "depends on how much you drink. Too much will produce a very uncivilized headache." She moved her face close and kissed him lightly on the lips.

"And that," Horn assessed, "is a very civilized kiss."

"A Sunday kiss."

"Look," he said, and pointed to the sky as a lone bird flew across the yellow sun to the south. "Don't see 'em that low too often."

"A vulture?"

"Not hardly. That's an eagle, a golden eagle, and there's a lot of difference."

"It's hard to tell from this distance."

"I suppose." Horn leaned on his elbow. "Most *people* look alike from a distance. Can't tell the buzzards from the eagles, the scavengers from the hunters. But nothing much gets close to an eagle unless the eagle comes after it."

"I've heard stories that they attack children."

"Not true — just stories. The eagle is nature's noblest bird, a true hunter. Vultures are scavengers. That's why they're built different."

"How different?"

"Vultures don't attack. They live off the dead. Don't have strong feet like the eagles, with sharp claws."

"Like the talon you're wearing around your neck?"

"That's right. One of the tools of the hunter. And eagles have hunters' eyes, placed forward and with telescopic vision."

"But the eagle kills, preys on other living things."

"Has to. That's part of nature."

"To kill?"

Horn pointed to the picnic basket. "Somebody did in that bird we just ate. Eagle's got to eat too, feed his young. And he's good at it. That's why he's got the Indians' respect. Indians put great store in eagles. Big medicine."

"Not just Indians," said Shana. "I remember in school that from ancient times the eagle was regarded as an almost mystical symbol in religion and mythology."

"I don't know about the mystical part, but it's the best hunter in the sky. Nature saw to that."

"When you say nature, you mean God."

"If you like, just so you remember sometimes nature's cruel — but it never lies. Only people can lie. It's something we managed to invent, like war and money."

"But we have to have money."

"Why?"

"Well, to buy things."

"Trouble is, people want too many things, things they don't really need. You see, an Indian, like all nature's other animals, will only kill as much as he needs to eat. But once you get civilized, you start to accumulate things, and if you have to lie and make war and cheat, well, you can just chalk that up to being civilized. Eagles and Indians are better off not civilized."

"What about scouts?" Shana smiled.

"I guess we're someplace in between." Horn shrugged. "But remember, I'm not a scout anymore."

"Aren't you?"

"Scouts don't go on picnics — or drink wine."

"You think you can get used to it?"

"The picnic part, not the wine. That's too civilized."

She came close again. This time it wasn't a Sunday kiss.

They didn't get back to Bowie until after dark.

Chapter 29

It was an early-August evening. Tom Horn prepared to close the store while Shana prepared dinner in the kitchen.

A stranger entered and looked the place over — not just looked, but assessed, evaluating the sight and even the scent of the establishment.

He looked as out of place as lace on a saddle blanket. The stranger was obviously a man of the East, a man of quality, if quality could be measured by manner and wardrobe. He wore an expression of genteel aloofness and a double-breasted, six-button blue suit exquisitely tailored to his tall but moderate measurement.

His was a handsome face, looking every month of its thirty-four years, with burnished eyes and hair to match, crowned by a color-coordinated Homburg. All this was framed by a terra-cotta cape hardly necessary on a warm summer night. His right hand brandished a pearl-handled malacca walking stick.

Tom Horn resisted his initial impulse to laugh or at least smile at this unique specimen of sartorial elegance in a place such as this.

"Evening," said Horn with a trace of amusement. "Is there something I can get for you?"

"Yes, there is," the stranger replied. "If she's on the premises, you can get me my fiancée."

Suddenly there was nothing amusing about the stranger.

Horn stood silent for a moment.

"I presume you're Tom Horn." The man spoke in a light, lilting, almost rhythmical tone. "I'm Brent Bradford, and I've come from Boston to see Shana. Would you be good enough to announce me?"

It wasn't necessary. Shana had heard Bradford's unmistakable voice. She now stood at the apartment doorway. If the ghost of Paul Revere had appeared she would not have been more surprised and startled. If Brent Bradford had meant to make an effective entrance, he could not have been more successful. He was on center stage and in complete command of the little drama. He caught sight of Shana at the doorway, removed his Homburg, went to her and kissed her with his thin dry lips before she recovered her composure.

"Shana, you were never lovelier — and in a kitchen apron. What a quaint touch! Aren't you going to say you're happy to see me?"

"Yes, of course, Brent. Of course. It's just that I'm so . . ."

"Pleased?"

"Well, yes, and surprised."

"Why should you be surprised? What's a four-thousand-mile odyssey to a man in love?" Bradford looked from Shana to Horn. "Isn't that so, Mr. Horn?"

"I wouldn't know," Horn replied.

"Oh? Pity. Well, if Helen could launch a thousand ships, why shouldn't Shana be responsible for a few railroad and stage-coach connections?"

Another moment as the silence built.

"Brent, you've met Tom. He's my . . . partner."

"We've not been formally introduced; however, Mr. Horn's reputation has assumed legendary proportions. Well, I hope you two are prospering."

"I was just closing up," said Horn. He picked up his hat. "Good night, Mr. . . ."

"Bradford," the banker replied.

"Tom, aren't you staying for supper?" Shana inquired awkwardly.

"You two'll have a lot to talk over. Good

night, Mr. Bradford. I hope you had a good trip."

"That," said Bradford, "has yet to be determined."

Tom Horn left without saying anything further.

"Big, handsome fellow, isn't he?" Bradford removed his cape and placed it, the cane, and Homburg on the counter. "Rather rough-hewn; seems somewhat anomolous in these surroundings. More suited to a livery stable, I'd say. But then you, too, look a little incongruous. Would you mind taking off that apron and greeting your fiancé in more suitable attire for the occasion?" Bradford took a small velvet jewelry box from his pocket, opened it, and displayed a large, sparkling diamond ring.

"Brent . . . !"

"Shana, apron and all I love you, intend to marry you and take you away from this musty, brummagem mercantile madness back to Boston and civilization."

"Brent, I had no idea you were so impetuous and . . . dashing."

"Oh, I can dash along with the best of them where you are concerned." He took the ring from its case and held it glittering between his thumb and forefinger. "I hope it's the right size. If not, we can have it adjusted back in Boston."

"I'm flattered that you've gone to all this trouble and expense; I really am, Brent — even fascinated. . . ."

"Good. Very good. I was hoping my unannounced appearance would have just such an effect."

"But I can't go back. Not now."

"Why not? Because of the imposing Mr. Horn? I'm sure he can make some other arrangement. The company won't be as good, but he'll find something else, somewhere else. He has that itinerant look about him. And you and I will settle by the bay and live happily ever after. How is that for a charming libretto?"

"But Brent, I have the store to —"

"Sell the store. I happen to know you have a buyer."

"How do you know?"

"Mr. Van Zeider wrote and told me."

Shana stiffened. At the mention of Van Zeider's name, Brent Bradford's journey came into focus. A lot of things came into focus. If the Machiavellian Karl Van Zeider couldn't get the store one way, he would find another. That other was Brent Bradford.

"What else did Mr. Van Zeider write and tell you?"

"Shana, look at me and listen carefully. This is the most important moment in both our lives." The look on Bradford's face and tone in his voice differed from the way Shana remembered the banker. He displayed an intensity she had thought him incapable of — even a strength. "I love you. I didn't know how much until you went away. I know you considered me something of a fop. I probably was and probably still am — but not as much of a fop as I used to be. I've never had a worry in the world, never wanted for anything. It was all there. Until you left. Then I realized the thing I wanted most was gone. Somehow that changed me, Shana. I'm not the same as I was before you left."

"Neither am I, Brent. I couldn't lie to you or try to deceive you. . . ."

"If it's about you and Horn, I don't want to hear. I'm not altogether naïve, and I can't pretend it didn't hurt at first. It still does. But the hurt doesn't matter or mean as much as you do. I love you and want you to be my wife. As for Mr. Horn, I've found out all about him. He's no more a merchant than you are. He's lived with savages because he, too, is a savage. And given half a chance he'll revert to that savagery. I don't want you to be here when he does.

What's happened, happened. What's going to happen is infinitely more important and lasting. I had to come and tell you that."

"Brent, you don't make it easy."

"I don't intend to. And in your heart you know you don't belong here with these people in this benighted place. The West isn't for everyone, and everyone isn't for the West. It might have sounded and seemed adventurous. Well, you've had your adventure, and I've had my awakening. I'm leaving tomorrow. I have to. There's a board of directors meeting soon, and I'm being named president of Bankers Trust. I don't expect you to come with me. But I'm leaving this." He placed the ring back in the case and put it on the counter. "I'll wait if it takes a month or a year or ten years. I love you Shana. We belong together."

He came to her and kissed her, this time with an intensity and strength she had never felt in him before. Still she didn't respond as she had with Tom Horn.

Bradford put on his hat, picked up his cape and cane, and started for the door. Even his step was different, more mature and assured.

"I'll be waiting, Shana," he said, and was gone.

It was nearly midnight.

Tom Horn sat at the table near the window in Van Zeider's *cantina*. Both elbows rested against the arms of the chair and his chin between his knuckles of both fists as he looked at the untouched whiskey bottle and shot glass in front of him.

There were a couple of the usual card games going on, and as usual Baldy and Peg, primed by the pump of conversation juice, were on either side of the bar philosophizing. Both Peg and Baldy cut their conversation to a standstill when they saw Shana Ryan enter, stand at the doorway, and look at Tom Horn.

Horn rose and went to her.

"Tom, I want to talk to you," she said softly.

"You shouldn't be in here."

"Then take me home."

Horn nodded and guided her to the door.

"Hey, Mr. Horn," Peg blurted, pointing toward the bottle on the table, "that jug's paid for."

"You drink it," Horn replied, and escorted Shana out of the *cantina*.

They walked for a way in silence toward the store.

"Tom, I want to tell you about Brent and me."

"Why aren't you with your fiancé? He came a long way for your company."

"He's not my fiancé — and Brent's leaving tomorrow."

"Are you going with him?"

"He asked me to."

"That figures."

"I'm not going. At least, not tomorrow."

"Why not?"

"A lot of reasons. I'm walking with one of them. Tom, I should have told you about him, but I thought that was all in the past."

"You don't owe me any explanations. I guess I'm the one doing the owing."

"Tom, he knows about us. *All* about us. I never thought he could accept something like that, but he's changed. I suppose we all have."

"Yeah. You. Me. Sieber. The Apache Kid. And him. It's been a long summer."

"I don't regret the 'you' and 'me.' "

"The time will come when you will, Shana. Maybe not tomorrow or soon, but sometime."

"I don't want to think about that, even if it's true. Right now I want things to go on just as they are."

They arrived at the front of the store.

"Thank you for bringing me home. And for this summer."

Horn said nothing.

"We're still partners," she added. "Will you be here tomorrow morning?"

"I will. Good night, Shana."

"Good night, darling." She unlocked the door and went inside.

Horn stood in the darkness. Some instinct told him that something was going to happen soon. Something that would change everything. Forever.

Chapter 30

The revealing dawn found the camp much as Horn had left it months ago, with both wickiups nestled against a sleeve of the Rincons near the stream that crept from the high country, drifted lazily past the flat of the camp, then meandered more quickly with the slanting terrain toward the valley below.

Old Pedro still lived in the smaller wickiup, and Suwan shared the larger with her son — Tom Horn's son. Before Horn left she had asked if he had a name he wanted their boy to be called. Tom had said no, so she chose Taw-Nee-Mara, "Spirit of the Wind." Tom Horn had agreed that it was a good name.

Pedro tickled Taw-Nee-Mara with a feather, and the baby gurgled and laughed. Suwan smiled as she fixed breakfast in the large wickiup. Pedro lifted the baby in his bony hands, and it gripped his thumbs and held on, swinging like a little monkey. Taw-Nee-Mara was long for his age and lithe, with his father's silver-blue eyes. His skin was coppery colored, much like his mother's, but with a little brass mixed in.

Suwan rose, picked up a bucket, and went outside. She walked as she did every morning toward the stream and listened to the sounds of early daylight. She knelt and swept her fingers through the cool green waters, then dipped both hands into the rivulet and splashed the liquid onto her face.

She wore a buckskin dress now and moccasins, but she remembered the times when she and Horn had swum naked in the cold autumn mornings and sometimes at night, when they would run without drying into the warm seclusion of the wickiup and lie together until they were dry.

Suwan had been with Apache braves before she became Horn's squaw. Apache braves took pride in the sexual powers of their manhood. Sex to an Apache was something to be taken — not given, or even shared. It was a thing to gratify the man. With the two Apache bucks, Suwan gave. But Horn showed her another side of sex. With him she didn't feel that she was being taken from — and she gave more in return.

Always she knew that he would leave. When they had been together she tried not to think of the time he would be gone. And when he left she tried not to wonder whether he would return. But she knew that if he did not come back by the first frost he would never be back, and she and Pedro and Taw-Nee-Mara would go to the reservation and live with the other Apaches.

She was thinking once more of Tom Horn as the strong, rude hand clapped over her mouth. She dropped the bucket. It hit a rock. Another hand grabbed her wrist and twisted her arm behind her. Suwan turned and looked into a face that she had never seen before — the face of the Apache Kid.

As the Kid pushed her forward, he heard a sound from the wickiup. He dropped his hand from her mouth, hooked and drew the Colt from its holster, and fired at the figure in the entrance of the wickiup.

Still holding the baby, Pedro saw the flash of the Colt, heard the blast, and felt the bullet tear through Taw-Nee-Mara and into his own chest.

As he fell into a deep black pit of unconsciousness, the last thing he heard was Suwan's scream.

Tom Horn was toting a hundred-pound sack of beans toward the wagon hitched in front of the store, when he saw the gaunt, blood-smeared old Indian, more dead than alive, straddling the pinto as it plodded into Fort Bowie.

A burlap sack was tied to the pommel of the saddle.

Tom Horn dropped the beans and ran toward old Pedro.

The compound was full of people watching, as Pedro slipped from the horse into Horn's arms.

Shana came from the store and stood next to Al Sieber, who was leaning on his crutches.

"Al, who is it?" she asked Sieber.

"It's one of Tom's . . . relatives," Sieber replied.

Horn gently lowered the Indian onto the ground and leaned close as Pedro whispered. He lived long enough to tell Horn what had happened. When there was nothing more to say or to live for, Pedro closed his eyes and died.

Tom Horn untied the burlap sack containing the body of his dead son from the saddle and carried it in both hands. He walked past Shana and Sieber without speaking.

At midnight Tom Horn still sat on the

straight-back chair in his room, looking at the naked body of the baby he had placed on his bed. There was a soft knock on the door.

"Who is it?"

"It's me, Tom," Shana's voice answered.

"Go away."

"Tom, let me come in, please."

"The door's not locked."

Shana entered. In her arms she carried infant's clothing and a small, soft white blanket. She stood silent in the darkness for a moment and looked at the broken, doll-like body on the bed.

"Al told me about you and Suwan and . . . the baby."

"I guess I should've told you, but I didn't. You had a right to know, and I'm sorry, if that's what you came to hear."

"That's not why I came. I brought some things — and a blanket."

"I'll bury him as he is — naked and bloody. That's the way I deserve to remember him."

"But what about *him*, Tom?"

"It doesn't make any difference to him."

"Please let me bathe him and —"

"Just leave the things here if you want. I'll take care of him."

"All right, Tom. Do you mind if Al and I

come along with you tomorrow?"

"Do what you will."

Shana placed the clothes and the blanket on the foot of the bed and left without another word.

Chapter 31

The hot summer wind quivered up from the south and blew a fine dust spray into Tom Horn's eyes as he put the last rock in place on the mound blanketing the grave of Taw-Nee-Mara.

Horn rose from his knees and walked away from the solitary sepulcher. He had not buried his son in a cemetery, but in the desert at the base of a cliff that rose like a cathedral, where the wind sang as it was singing now — a requiem for the innocent.

Horn reached the buggy where Shana and Sieber sat waiting. Pilgrim stood nearby.

"I'm sorry, Tom," Shana said, "truly sorry."

Horn wiped the wind-blown dirt from his eyes.

"His name was Spirit of the Wind," said Horn, "and that's where he is now." Horn mounted. "Well, Al, you're going to get what you wanted. I'm going after him. And I'm going to kill him."

"This isn't the way I wanted it."

"I know that — and if I had gone sooner

it wouldn't have happened this way."

"Tom," Shana implored, "let the troopers go with you."

Horn wheeled his horse around and without looking back — rode.

Shana placed her hand on Al Sieber's battered fist.

"He'll come back," said Sieber.

"Even if he does," Shana said softly, "he'll never be the same."

The Apache Kid had been without a squaw for almost a month when he took Suwan from the camp and left Pedro and the baby for dead. Suwan had started to run toward her fallen grandfather and Taw-Nee-Mara, but the Kid had grasped her wrist, twisted her to him, and hit her across the head with the barrel of his gun.

She became aware of the ground moving under her and realized she had been bound hand and foot by thong and slung belly-down over the saddle of the Kid's Appaloosa. The Kid straddled the back of the animal just behind the saddle. Suwan, her head throbbing from the blow of the gun barrel, did her best to pretend she was still unconscious, but the Kid knew the moment her eyes opened, even though he didn't see them.

He chose a ridge along the river, with broken boulders, cottonwoods, and soft, damp grass. The Apache Kid dismounted under the shade of a tree, then roughly pulled Suwan from the saddle onto the ground. The Kid dug his moccasins under her midsection and rolled her over on her back. She knew there was no use pretending she was unconscious. Suwan opened her eyes and saw the Apache Kid holding a knife and kneeling toward her. He cut her legs free of the thongs, then her wrists.

Without speaking, his face told her what would come next and how it would be. She knew if she resisted it would be worse.

She didn't resist.

Tom Horn knew that the place to begin would be the most painful, but he went back to the camp where he and Suwan had lived.

He set aside the pain. He would have to set aside all emotion that might dull or drain his searcher's senses and instincts.

He was a hunter now; a hunter tracking a wild animal that he would kill — or it would kill him.

Horn dismounted and read much of what had happened. The bucket near the stream where Suwan had knelt. The signs of struggle. The shooting. The hoofprints of the shod Appaloosa, heavier now with an added burden. The tracks, leading into the stream and being swallowed by the running water.

Horn nudged Pilgrim into the stream and followed its course. There were a hundred places to emerge without leaving tracks. It was impossible for Horn, patient as he was, to determine which of these the Kid had chosen. Horn would have to leave the stream and begin the circle — ever widening until he read some sign of the Kid and Suwan.

But there were no signs.

General Miles had ordered Crane and the others to continue the patrols in search of the Apache Kid. Maybe Horn would find the renegade and maybe he wouldn't but it would be better for Miles's record if the United States Army under his command found the renegade first.

The face of the jackrabbit blended into the brush. Only the eyes moved — almost imperceptibly. Then the head turned, reacting to something, and the rabbit sprinted away.

The bullet kicked up a wad of dirt just in

front of the jack, and the frenzied little animal changed directions. The second bullet hit its mark, smacking the rabbit off its feet. The jack twisted into the air and landed dead on the sage.

The Apache Kid, on horseback, lowered the rifle; then his foot nudged Suwan, who stood nearby. The Kid's head motioned toward the rabbit about forty feet away. Suwan seemed in a trance but turned and walked toward the dead animal.

As she came to the thicket where the rabbit lay, the Kid followed on horseback some distance behind. Suwan stooped to retrieve the rabbit but was arrested by the sight of a rattler, coiled and ready to strike. At first her eyes were hypnotized by the spiraled creature, but then they flicked back toward the Kid, who was reloading the Winchester.

Suwan snapped out of her trance and snatched up the now-rattling serpent. It struck and missed as the squaw hurled the snake like a deadly bola toward the Kid. But the Kid saw and heard and fired sending a bullet into the rattler, decapitating it in midflight.

Suwan stared at the Kid in silence and waited.

The Kid shoved the Winchester into its

boot, then urged the Appaloosa toward Suwan, looking as if he might kill her. Instead, he leaned low and picked up the dead jack by its ears, then nudged the woman with his foot, pointing north.

Suwan began to walk, followed by the Kid on horseback.

The Apache Kid hunkered near the small smokeless campfire, roasting the jack. Suwan sat, leaning against a tree that sheltered the fire. She stared into the elfish flames. All day through the relentless summer sun she had been walking, past the point of exhaustion.

The Kid tore a strip of flesh from the rabbit and ate. He nodded permission for her to eat. Suwan neither moved nor reacted. He finished chewing, then tore another ribbon of rabbit and move nearer, holding the meat close to her face. She turned away.

His left hand grasped her face like a claw squeezing her jaw open, and he thrust the food into her mouth. She spat the meat back at him, and his fist slammed in the side of her face. She fell unconscious, almost into the fire.

The Kid pulled her by the hair away from the flames, then cut another slice from the roasting rabbit and ate.

Miles away, Tom Horn had made dry camp. He unsaddled Pilgrim, rubbed down the animal, fed him some grain and water, ate a meager meal, and laid his head on the blanket roll. He looked up at the stars piercing the deep blue sky and winking a million miles away.

Horn closed his eyes. He thought of the farm in Missouri, of the times on the trail with Sieber, of Geronimo in faraway Florida, of Shana and the bed they had shared but once, of the grave that forever imprisoned Taw-Nee-Mara, and of the Apache Kid with Taw-Nee-Mara's mother.

It was the heart of the night's darkness. The campfire was silent and cold, only ashes, mixed with the bones of the rabbit. The Apache Kid slept with rifle under him and gun in hand. Suwan lay near him, her anguished eyes open in her swollen face, but unmoving. Then slowly, slowly, she looked toward him and away again.

After he struck her unconscious he had taken the dress off her and placed it with the rifle under him where he slept. Naked except for her moccasined feet, Suwan moved first one leg, then the other. Silent as a blush, she managed to rise, then froze until she was sure the Kid still slept. With slow, unheard steps, she crept past the pool of cold gray ashes, then disappeared around a rock and breathed for the first time but still without sound.

Suwan made her way into a dark miniature ravine, then moved faster as she breathed an audible breath and ran into the hollow black night. Faster around another turn, across a gully, faster over the crooked trunk of a fallen dead tree, faster around a bell-shaped boulder — and directly into the waiting form of the Apache Kid.

Suwan screamed, but the Kid clutched her throat and forced the scream into silence and Suwan onto her knees. Just when it seemed he would choke the life out of her body, he relaxed his hand, and she fell, a limp, dim outline on the ground. The Kid reached under her armpit and forced her to her feet. He pushed her roughly in the direction of the camp. Somehow, half-stumbling, half-crawling, she made it like a spent dog back to the camp, where she lay on her naked belly and bruised face. But the long night's ordeal was only beginning.

The Apache Kid reached down and turned her on her back.

Chapter 32

Shana Ryan stood behind the counter sipping a cup of after-breakfast coffee as Sergeant Cahill, Trooper Dawson, and two other troopers, MacLeod and Keller, entered the store.

"Payday this morning, Miss Ryan," Cahill announced. "We'd like to settle our accounts for the month, ma'am."

"All right," said Shana, riffling through a stack of slips near the cash register as the men produced money. "Cahill, nine sixty-five."

"Here's ten even, ma'am. Hold on to the change," Cahill grinned. "I want to keep my credit good."

"Your credit's always good, Sergeant," Shana smiled. "Dawson — eight fifty. MacLeod — ten seventy-five. Keller — eight ninety."

The troopers all put money down. Each followed Cahill's example and made Shana keep the change to the next dollar.

"Any word from ol' Tom?" Cahill inquired as Shana tore up the monthly credit slips.

"No, nothing. Will you men want anything else this morning?"

"No, ma'am," said Dawson. "Just thought we'd better square up before we charged the *cantina*."

"I'll take a plug of tobacco," said Cahill. "Pay cash money."

As Shana carried out the transaction, Captain Crane came in through the open door. The troopers tossed him a perfunctory salute and walked onto the porch, but heard the beginning of the conversation that followed.

"Good morning, Captain." Then Shana asked immediately, "Did the patrol find any . . . ?"

"No, no sign of either one of them in almost two weeks," said Crane. "Not a campfire, not a track, not a scratch or a scent. It's as if they've both evaporated."

Outside, the troopers lingered on the porch. They knew the *cantina* wouldn't open for another quarter of an hour.

"I'll bet ol' Horn brings back the Kid's scalp in his saddlebag," said Cahill, biting into the tobacco plug.

"Not likely," Keller replied. "The Kid ain't human."

"Neither's Horn," Cahill observed. "He'll get the Kid if he has to track him from soda to hock, follow him from this world right into the next."

"If he does find him, I don't reason Horn'd kill him," MacLeod ventured. "Hell, them two shared the same canteen too long."

"Yeah, well now," Keller grinned, "the Kid's sharing Horn's squaw. I'll bet Horn blows his eyeballs out, both of 'em."

Shana had come close to the open door and heard what the troopers were saying.

"Besides, there's the reward," Cahill retorted. "I got a double eagle that says Horn hangs him up to dry."

"I'll take that bet," MacLeod said.

"I'll put ten on Horn," Dawson added.

"You're covered!" Keller exclaimed, and as he did a crutch smashed across his back and head, propelling the would-be gambler off the porch, into the hitching post, and onto the ground.

Sieber stood on his remaining crutch, his face a thundercloud. Captain Crane moved past Shana and through the doorway.

"I think you men better pick up your friend," Crane suggested, "and go do a little drinking."

The suggestion was greeted by a chorus of "Yessir's" as the troopers lifted up

Keller and dragged him in the direction of the *cantina.*

"Good morning, Al," Crane greeted the old scout, then walked off across the compound.

Al Sieber hobbled into the store, using the surviving crutch and whatever other support was available along the way, until he reached a half barrel and sat. Shana refrained from trying to assist him.

"I don't blame you," she said, carrying in the remnants of the broken crutch. "Betting as if it were some game. It's uncivilized."

"It's nature's game," Sieber said slowly. "And no, it ain't civilized. Never has been."

"What do you mean?" Shana leaned back on the counter.

"I mean it's nature's bible. Since the beginning there's been the hunter and the hunted. But nature provides a difference between the two. Trouble is — there ain't no difference between those two."

"Of course there is." Now she leaned forward.

"Not the way I mean," said Sieber. "In nature's contest the hunted is usually small, fast, and hard to spot. The hunter's strong and equipped with tooth and claw.

271

But those two got the same equipment."

"Oh, Al," she sighed, "if he hadn't gone alone, maybe . . ."

"No." Sieber shook his head. "That's the way to do it. The Kid can spot a flea in a herd of buffalo. Alone's the way. I've gone over it a thousand times. The way I'd do it if I was either one, the hunter or the hunted."

The old scout had silently played out the pursuit over and over to himself. Now for the first time he gave expression to his thoughts. "The hunted's got things in his favor: space, places to hide, room to get lost — every coulee, every draw, every rise, every depression, every turn, tree, and rock gives him cover. And if the hunter misses him once, he might never find him again.

"But even the hunted has to eat. Food is where you find it, and the Kid knows where — and how. Quail, rabbit, field mice, maybe a prairie dog in the desert.

"And in the mountain flanks, acorns — and there's Spanish bayonet. The Kid might roast some mescal — tastes good, but you can smell it downwind. If the going gets really tough, there's the gum of the mesquite or the inner bark of pine. So the Kid could eat, all right. And so could Tom. He knows every trick of the Apache.

"A hunter like Tom Horn who's a patient man has time on his side. And Horn knows how to see without being seen. He can read every track on the trail, mark on the grass, scratch on the bark of a tree, and he can tell nearly to the hour how long ago it was made . . . and by what.

"Did the animal Tom spotted on the trail see what Tom's looking for? Well, there's no way of telling that. But sooner or later even an animal smart as the Kid has to leave something behind. And sooner or later Horn'll find it — the link that says, 'What you're looking for passed this way.'

"If the Kid's still got the squaw with him, it'll be that much easier for Tom.

"So chances are, Horn'll find the Kid. But finding him's one thing. Up to now the Kid doesn't know Horn is dogging him. When he finds out, there's no way of telling the outcome. They both got the same equipment . . . and every living thing wants to go on living. That's the first commandment of nature's bible."

Chapter 33

It was as Sieber described to Shana Ryan — the Kid and Suwan always on the move, with the Apache Kid making sure that no evidence of their existence was left behind. He covered the ashes of their camps and even buried the waste from their bodies.

On horseback, the Kid moved in the middle of every stream, hunched in the cavity of a rock as the rain of a summer storm cascaded off the crag, doubled back across the forlorn desert, then headed into the high country, where he could survey the landscape from every approach.

Suwan knew what would befall her when the Kid made camp each night. Her buckskin dress had become a tattered rag. Somehow she clung to the faintest of hopes, an unreasonable hope, that Horn had heard about Taw-Nee-Mara and Pedro and would decide to come after their son's killer. She had little illusion about her own worth to him, but Horn might come after the baby's murderer.

Even if he did come, and as good a tracker as Suwan knew Horn to be, the

Kid was making sure no tracker could follow.

Wherever possible, when she knew the Kid was occupied, Suwan would tear a tiny fragment from her dress and leave it, almost invisible, in the grass, on the bank of a stream, or in the crevice of a rock that pointed to the high country.

But the Kid's one mistake, one careless moment, had come early, when Suwan flung the rattler at his face.

It took time, crossing, crisscrossing, and doubling back, but as Sieber had said, Horn finally found a sign.

Tom Horn picked it up — the ejected shell from the Apache Kid's rifle. He walked a few steps and stopped, his foot near the dried-up head of a snake. Nearby, he spotted the rest of the rattler's remains. That was the beginning.

They were in the high country when the Apache Kid looked back and saw her fall exhausted against a rock and then onto the hard ground. He knew that he would have to get himself another companion. This one was of no further service. She was now a handicap, a useless burden.

The Apache Kid dismounted. He began to walk toward her, then paused and took a couple of steps in the opposite direction. He stopped at the edge of the tabletop precipice that plunged into a bottomless canyon.

He stood at the brink of the escarpment and looked down at the slash of jagged canyon, then back at the crumpled form of the squaw. He started toward her.

Suwan was bruised, barely conscious, and without strength as the Kid reached down, took hold of her arm, and dragged her toward the rim of the plateau.

At the lip of the precipice the Kid dropped her limp arm. As he moved his foot under the flesh of her belly to kick her over the cliff, the gunshot thundered, its echo reverberated, and the bullet burned through the husk of the Kid's leg.

The Apache Kid wheeled and went for his holster but heard the click as Horn cocked the hammer of his Colt and pointed it at the Kid's heart. There was a moment of silence as the hunter and the hunted faced each other.

"You got careless," Horn said finally.

"Yeah." It was the first word the Kid had spoken since he left Fort Bayard. And for the first time the expression in his eyes changed, softened. His eyes, face, and attitude were almost like those of the easygoing, happy kid that Horn once called brother. The Kid nodded toward Suwan and smiled. "I shoulda shed her sometime back."

The Kid wiped the blood from his leg — slowly, to reassure Tom Horn that he was not making a play for his gun.

"What the hell did you go and do that for?" the Kid asked as he held up his stained hand.

"Unbuckle the gunbelt," was Horn's answer. "Left hand."

The Kid's smile diminished a trace as he unbuckled the gunbelt and let it drop near the edge of the cliff.

"Tom," he said, "I ain't ever seen your hand . . . unsteady before."

Horn's hand was unmistakably trembling — slightly, but trembling. He was not the cold complete hunter now. He was human. So was the Apache Kid, even if he had killed and pillaged like a wild animal. Horn looked at Suwan as she stirred.

"She was 'most dead," the Kid shrugged. "I was just gonna put her out of her misery."

Suwan, a gaunt, almost unrecognizable relic of the glistening-skinned, gleaming-eyed beauty she had been, managed to raise her bruised face and look toward Horn.

"Suwan . . ." Horn said.

"You know this one?" The Apache Kid was surprised and at the same time disappointed.

"And I knew our son, too," Horn answered.

"Awww *hell*, Tom," the Kid shrugged, "I didn't know." Then he looked into Horn's haunted eyes and smiled, "But that don't exactly cover you with glory either."

"No," said Horn hoarsely. "It don't."

"What are you gonna do, Tom?" The Kid thought he was gaining the advantage. "Take me all the way back to Bowie to stand trial?"

"I'm not sure I could get you back."

"Neither am I," the Kid smiled.

"So you're standing trial right here, Kid," said Horn. "I'm the judge and jury . . ."

"Awww, come on, Tom."

"and," Horn finished, "the executioner."

"You mean that?"

"I'm gonna kill you, Kid."

"Are you?" The Apache Kid wiped more of the blood from his leg. "You had the chance. Why didn't you do it?"

"I wanted you to know it was me."

278

With his left hand the Kid tore the thong from his neck and held out the eagle claw.

"What about this . . . brother?" The Kid hollered. "Remember Sibi's Boys?"

"You broke that to a finish when you shot him."

"I could've killed him, and you know it. But I didn't."

"You've killed everything."

"I saved your hide more than once, brother. It was Sieber's leg or my life, and you know that, too."

"I know that you don't deserve to live, not after killing innocent men and after what you've done to her" — Horn looked at Suwan then back to the Kid — "and others like her."

"I needed . . . company," the Kid smiled. "You know how it is."

"No, I don't. Not like that. And there was a time you wouldn't have either. You killed everything that stood in the way —"

"The way to white man's jail and justice! It was them or me! Not much of a choice when you happen to be me. Sieber said it: 'Every living thing wants to go on living.' Well, I'd rather live a month out here than twenty years in Yuma."

"You're going to die out here," Horn said, not wanting to hear any more, not wanting to take the chance, remote as it was, that the Kid might build a defense for his indefensible, reprehensible crimes. As if to reinforce his own resolve, Horn looked again at Suwan, the incontrovertible victim of the Apache Kid's inhumanity.

She lifted her blurry eyes and realized that her last faint, hopeless hope had somehow materialized — that Taw-Nee-Mara's father had followed and stood with gun in hand pointed at the murderer of their son.

"Tow-Kee-Low." With lips parched and cracked, she hoarsely whispered Horn's Apache name.

Still covering the Apache Kid with his Colt, Horn walked to the Kid's horse, un-looped the canteen, and went to the girl. The Kid didn't move, only watched.

Horn unscrewed the cap of the canteen with the gun still pointed at the Kid. Suwan whispered something. Horn leaned closer to hear. Suwan tried to smile and muttered that she knew he would come — and then it happened.

The Kid leaped like a cougar and crashed into Horn, knocking the Colt loose from his hand and catapulting the canteen over the edge of the cliff.

This, too, was as Sieber had prophesied

— a conflict between two animals provided by nature with the same equipment. It was brutal, bloody, beastly, with sounds of broken flesh and cartilage, hammering knuckles, ripping elbows, exploding kicks, and crushing head butts.

It was not a fight, but a struggle to maim, to hurt, to survive. It was two primitive brutes peeling away the layers of civilization, repudiating all rules, and reverting to the earth's dawn, when the fundamental instinct was to kill and avoid being killed.

They fell tangled to the ground, their battered faces an inch apart, eye to eye, with every bone, fiber, and muscle straining.

Suwan summoned a last ounce of ebbing strength and inched her hand closer to the Kid's discarded gunbelt. Her quivering fingers closed around the curve of the gun butt and withdrew it from the holster.

The Kid was gaining advantage over Horn. He saw the gun and the movement of Suwan's arm. The Kid's fist bolted into Horn's chin, and he leaped feet first toward the gun aimed at him. Both feet slammed into Suwan, hurtling her and the gun over the precipice and down the rock wall of the canyon.

At the same moment Horn was upon the

Kid, twisting him and smashing a fist full strength into the Indian's face while losing his own balance. The impact knocked the Kid over the edge, but he managed a desperate hold on Horn's hand, pulling him onto the ground and almost over the side.

The Kid dangled on the face of the cliff, still clinging to Horn's hand, which was now clamped around the Kid's wrist, with death beckoning below.

The Apache Kid's face was a ghostly, broken basilisk, a garish mask. He said nothing, but his eyes pleaded, maybe even prayed, as they stared up at Horn, who looked into the face of his "brother."

The Kid could hold on no longer. But Horn's grip was still firm.

The Apache Kid smiled — maybe because he thought Horn would pull him up, maybe because he knew it was all over and this was his last defiance.

Tom Horn let go and watched the Apache Kid fall, twisted and torn and smashed into eternity.

For a long time Horn looked down through eyes scarred by memories. He relived the times of triumph and tears, laughter and disappointment, serenity and torment, rapture and regret with both Suwan and the Apache Kid. Then Tom Horn rolled over on the top of the plateau, and his face rested near the broken thong with the Apache Kid's eagle claw.

Chapter 34

Storm clouds swirled across the night's blue awning above Fort Bowie and pressed down past the towering peaks onto the mass of slanting earth below. Thunder roared, reinforcing the threat, and the warning became a reality with lightning and then rain, warm rain driven by the wind onto the face of the land. The rain pelted the canyon cliffs and ridges, then the flatlands and basins, and flowed onto the dark, thirsty desert.

But General Nelson Appleton Miles would not let a little wetness dampen the evening's celebration in honor of his wife's recent arrival at Fort Bowie. He had planned a party, and General Miles seldom deviated from plan.

Mary Miles was a handsome woman, large boned but with patrician features and with more passion than Miles had expected before they married. And always after their long separations, she ardently reminded him what a hot-blooded woman he had married. Miles looked forward to the physical facet of their relationship and just as eagerly to another aspect of their alliance: Mary was his best and certainly most appreciative audience and admirer. She believed what he believed — that Nelson Appleton Miles was the finest, brightest, most capable officer in uniform and that one day, deservedly so, he would become Commander in Chief of the United States Army. But they both knew that his rise to command would depend on political as well as military campaigns.

Years ago, when Crook won his brigadier's star, Miles had been bitter with jealousy, and so was Mary. Miles wrote Sherman that the promotion should have gone to him, as so did Mary.

Miles always believed that the fraternity of West Pointers invariably stuck together and looked upon him as an alien. Miles, in his early twenties, had been a dry-goods clerk when the Civil War erupted. He purchased a commission and discovered his life's profession. The army suited him better than clerking and provided greater opportunities for advancement, especially when he made Mary his life's partner.

Through the years she gloried in watching and listening to him, and he reveled in posturing and posing in front of her and relating all the past triumphs and predicting all the future victories that would be emblazoned on the Miles escutcheon.

When the faithful General was absent, he wrote long, detailed letters almost every night to remind her of his ardor and ambition. Mary needed no reminder of either, but she read, reread, and treasured the letters and had them bound into a book for handy reference to review when he was on campaign.

But now they were together, and both had much to celebrate. Word was already circulating in Washington, disseminated by well-placed proponents and relatives, that General Miles had succeeded at long last where all the other generals had failed, in resolving the Apache problem. He had succeeded from both a military and an administrative point of view. There was even talk of nominating him as a vice-presidential candidate. Neither the general nor his wife found objection to that office, for the time being. Of course, Washington hadn't heard about a lone Indian called the Apache Kid or a scout named Tom Horn. Secretly Miles hoped that he would never hear from or about either of them again.

While a dozen couples danced, the orchestra in the gaily decorated hall at Fort Bowie played waltzes occasionally punctuated by thuds of thunder and cracks of lightning against the persistent accompaniment of drumming rain.

All the officers were resplendent in their smartest uniforms, and the ladies featured their finest gowns. Most resplendent was General Miles, at the head of a reception line near the door. At least he was modest enough to draw the line at wearing his gold sword. Mrs. Miles, handsome and adoring as ever, smiled and nodded next to her Napoleon.

Al Sieber sat across the room with his crutches between his legs. Van Zeider was at the punch bowl, as was Doctor Jedadiah Barnes in a laundered shirt and a semiwrinkled black suit, and next to him stood Nurse Thatcher, straight as a scalpel in a starched white gown. She sipped blood-red punch from a crystal glass.

"Go ahead," Barnes commented to her. "Drink it and you'll look just like a thermometer."

"You can go to hell, you old beaver," she replied. "I'm not on duty tonight."

Those still entering were drenched from the unrelenting downpour. The men's slickers and the ladies' coats were taken by Sergeant Cahill and Trooper Dawson just inside the door as the arrivals proceeded toward General and Mrs. Miles.

Captain Crane and Shana Ryan entered together, offered their wet outerwear to the soldiers, and advanced to be received by their hosts.

"Miss Ryan," the General smiled, "I'd like to present my wife."

"Welcome to Fort Bowie, Mrs. Miles." Shana also smiled.

"Thank you, Miss Ryan," Mrs. Miles replied, and added to all the smiles.

The General motioned. "Mary, you know Captain Crane. He's been of some help here."

Crane nodded courteously, acknowledging Miles's generous accolade.

"Will you be staying here permanently, Mrs. Miles?" Shana inquired.

"I'll be staying as long as Nelson does." The gowned woman glowed toward her mate. "But now that he's made this place safe, I suppose they'll give him a command at some other trouble spot."

"Yes, well" — Miles cleared his throat, if not his conscience, and indicated the dance floor — "you two enjoy yourselves. We'll chat later on."

Crane and Shana both accepted the polite dismissal. They noticed Nurse Thatcher accompanied by Doctor Barnes who carried an extra glass of punch while walking toward Sieber. Shana and the captain joined the procession and exchanged greetings with the doctor, the nurse, and the old scout.

"Here, Al," said Doctor Barnes, extending the extra glass to Sieber. "Have some of this stuff, it'll mix real good with that tobacco. Hatchet here's swallowed half a bucket already. How's the leg?"

"Can't you see?" Sieber took the glass and pointed toward the crutches. "I'm completely recovered."

"I'd say in a month or so," Barnes diagnosed, "you'll be trading them in for a walking stick, something that looks like Hatchet here, only shorter."

"It's Thatcher, and I'm sorry you asked me to come along, you old cockroach."

"I *said* Thatcher, and I didn't ask you, you asked me. I wonder if that orchestra knows 'Forty Shades of Green.' "

"Can I get you a glass of punch, Shana?" Crane inquired.

"Thank you," she replied. She noticed Karl Van Zeider nodding charmingly in her direction. Van Zeider had dropped by the store from time to time during Horn's absence, made a few purchases he probably didn't need, and indulged in polite conversation about everything except

289

Horn, Bradford, and another offer. But she knew that he was a patient as well as a persistent man. He would play the waiting game, waiting for the possibility of her accepting Bradford's marriage proposal, for Horn to kill the Apache Kid or vice versa — or better yet, both. Shana returned Van Zeider's nod and quickly averted his gaze.

It seemed that all the guests had arrived — at least, those who mattered. General and Mrs. Miles moved away from the entrance onto the dance floor.

"Would you care to dance?" Crane asked Shana as they finished their drinks.

"Yes, I would," Shana smiled. "But you know, Captain, I haven't danced since I left Boston."

"Well, I'm a lot rustier than that," said Crane, "so come along at your own risk."

They waltzed onto the floor and danced as perfectly as if they had been going to cotillion together for years.

"Mrs. Miles is a beautiful woman," said Shana.

"Yes," Crane agreed, "but she certainly has a blind spot."

"What do you mean?"

"A wife should be in love with her husband but, Mrs. Miles thinks the general is the be-all and the end-all."

"And you don't?"

"I'm going to ask for a transfer . . ." Crane hesitated. ". . . as soon as . . ."

"As what? Oh! You mean when Tom . . . comes back?"

"Yes."

"I guess a lot depends on that," Shana reflected, "for Mr. Sieber and . . ."

"And you?" Crane looked into her eyes, but Shana didn't answer.

There was a great roar of thunder and the electric crack of lightning, as if the bolt had just missed the building. At that instant the door was flung open, and framed on the threshold with rain and lightning behind him was the ghostlike figure of Tom Horn.

He stood like some half-crazed creature out of a wild Walpurgis Night, with wet, swollen face and grave-digger eyes. He wore no coat. His shirt was torn and mudcaked.

Every eye turned upon him. The waltzers stopped waltzing. The orchestra stopped playing. Al Sieber rose on his crutches, but no one else moved. No one except Tom Horn.

He closed the door and stepped forward, walking not fast, not slow, toward Sieber, who waited. Horn moved past Shana. She took a step, but went no closer. At least he had come back; he was alive — with worn-out eyes and blood-matted hair, bruised and beaten but alive. Shana told herself that nothing else mattered.

"Nelson," Mrs. Miles whispered as Horn passed, "who is that . . . man?"

Miles just stood, a portrait of command indecision.

Tom Horn stopped in front of Sieber. Their eyes locked for a moment. Then Horn raised his right hand, opened his fist, and placed the Apache Kid's eagle claw in the old scout's gnarled hand.

Sieber nodded. He understood.

Horn turned and started to leave.

"It's the Kid's!" Sergeant Cahill pointed to the talon in Sieber's hand. "Horn got the Apache Kid! I told you he'd bring him to his milk!"

Soldiers and civilians moved closer to get a look at the claw, as if they were viewing the remains of the Apache Kid.

Doctor Barnes stepped in front of Horn and pressed his arm. "You need some attention, boy. You look half-dead, and it ain't easy to tell which half."

Horn shook his head and moved off. As he did, Cahill hollered out, "Congratulations, Tom! You got the reward coming!

292

Six thousand dollars!"

Horn kept walking, but now Karl Van Zeider blocked his way.

"Just a minute," Van Zeider protested. "That trinket doesn't prove a thing. This is a trick to collect the reward." He thrust a finger near Horn's face and demanded, "Where's the body, Mr. Horn? Where is the *body?*"

Horn lashed out with the same savagery he had fought the Kid. He held on to Van Zeider and smashed blow after blow onto the man's face.

Van Zeider would have fallen after the first blow, but Horn held him up with one hand and continued hitting him with the other until they both fell on top of the punch-bowl table, collapsing everything on it. Horn, now certainly a madman, kept on beating his fists into Van Zeider's body and face amidst the broken table, crystal bowl, and glasses.

Cahill, Dawson, Crane, and a half dozen other troopers stormed at Horn and finally managed to pull him off and pinion him. Horn could barely stand, but his eyes still blazed with unsatisfied vengeance at the inert figure on the floor.

"Get that maniac out of here!" General Miles commanded.

Horn's eyes, lizard cold, looked at Miles, then at the men holding him. He was now in control of himself. As his body relaxed they let go of him.

He walked alone past the still-stunned spectators, who stood like statues. Shana was near the door staring at him. He stopped and looked at her for the first time. There was a fervid look in her eyes he had never seen before.

"You're as much a savage as he was," she said.

Tom Horn opened the door and walked out into the rain.

Chapter 35

A lingering summer wind held the first hint of autumn, along with the faint taste of last night's rain. The clear Arizona air, scented by late-blooming flowers, foretold that soon summer would pass and other things with it. The waning year would give way to winter as time was giving way gradually to a new century and new ways.

The question was whether the West had been won — or defeated. The outlook depended on whether you were white or red, on whether you had been one who survived with the endless stretch of wagon trains that lumbered out of Kansas and Missouri — or whether you were bleached bones in the desert. It depended on whether you rode with Crook at Salt River Canyon or Custer at Little Big Horn. Not just the strong survived, but also the cunning, the careful, and the just plain lucky. Those at Fort Bowie this mordant morning had survived — at least so far.

There were as many people around as usual, but they were somehow more quiet than usual, and their attention if not their eyes angled toward Tom Horn as he strapped the saddlebags on Pilgrim's back.

"The trouble is," Doctor Jedadiah Barnes said to Nurse Thatcher while they watched through the window, "the Apache Kid was an Indian who thought he could live as a white man, and Tom Horn is a white man who tried to live like an Indian."

"Was that really so bad?" Nurse Thatcher asked.

"No, it wasn't bad," Doctor Barnes reflected. "Maybe it was just too soon."

Tom Horn still showed the marks of the fight with the Apache Kid. There was also a mark on his manner that showed as he tied the bedroll on the animal.

Shana approached. "Tom, I'm sorry for what I said last night."

"It doesn't matter." He did not look at her.

"Don't you care enough to make it matter?"

Horn didn't answer.

"Don't you?" she repeated.

"Not now," said Horn as he saddled up.

She felt everything slipping away — her illusions about the West, her outlook on life and love, the passion of summer's muffled night dispelled by the cold, angry dawn, the promises of unbound youth fettered by the heavy chains of reality, almost as real and heavy as those that girdled Geronimo. Maybe Brent Bradford had been right, at least about one thing: the West was not for everyone, and everyone was not for the West. Shana tried to cling to a last desperate hope like a fluttering bird fighting a wild wind.

"Tom," she asked, "will you come back?"

"No."

"What about your interest in the store?"

"I'm just not a storekeeper. Give my share to Sieber if you want."

Without goodbye, without looking back, he directed his animal toward the fort entrance. He remembered his words to Shana — that it wouldn't be easy to leave her. It wasn't easy. But Horn believed it was best, at least for her. There was a part of him forever sealed off — a territory within him wild and uncharted, pulling him across the next horizon toward the distant mountains. Without that part he could not be a husband. The Apaches were in chains now or confined to reservations, but the Apache part of Tom Horn was still free.

Out of a discolored, distorted face, Karl Van Zeider watched through the *cantina* window. He was already making plans.

With Horn gone, those plans would come to fruition much sooner and easier. Van Zeider would survive — and prevail. He felt the strength and ambition returning to his battered body, and his aching brain surged with confidence in the future.

General Miles and Mary stood on the headquarters porch along with Captain Crane. Horn approached but looked straight ahead.

"Nelson," Mrs. Miles inquired, "was that man in your army?"

"No, no, Mary," General Nelson Appleton Miles replied. "He was just a scout."

Captain Crane's look was one of unqualified disgust. He moved away from his superior and walked toward Horn, who now rode by. The captain threw a salute to the scout. Horn kept riding.

Al Sieber leaned on his crutches near the fort entrance. Here Horn paused.

"Where to?" Sieber asked.

"Miles was right about one thing," Horn shrugged, "the day of the scout is over — at least around here." Horn's face was calm, his voice even. "Might head up toward the Platte."

Al Sieber knew he was saying goodbye to his other son. He looked at Horn, and his eyes swam with memories. "If you run across Crook, well . . ."

"Yeah. Take care of yourself, Al. . . ." Tom Horn tore the thong and eagle claw from his neck and handed it to Sieber. "And this."

That was it. Horn started to ride away. Shana Ryan came and stood next to the old scout.

Sieber looked at Tom Horn riding away from Fort Bowie. The chief of scouts took something from his pocket, and his eyes went down to the beaten-up old hand.

It was open now, and in the creased and callused palm were two eagle claws. "Sibi's Boys," he whispered.

About the Author

Andrew J. Fenady created, wrote and produced the successful television series *The Rebel* and *Branded*. His work on *Hondo* led to a long and happy association with John Wayne that culminated in Fenady's writing and producing *Chisum*. In between stints at the desert film locations that have been Mr. Fenady's stamping ground, he has found time to write two highly acclaimed crime novels: *The Man with Bogart's Face* and *The Secret of Sam Marlow*. Andrew Fenady lives in Los Angeles with his wife and six children, and spends as much time as possible on his ranch near Palm Springs.

The employees of Thorndike Press hope you have enjoyed this Large Print book. All our Thorndike and Wheeler Large Print titles are designed for easy reading, and all our books are made to last. Other Thorndike Press Large Print books are available at your library, through selected bookstores, or directly from us.

For information about titles, please call:

(800) 223-1244

or visit our Web site at:

www.gale.com/thorndike
www.gale.com/wheeler

To share your comments, please write:

Publisher
Thorndike Press
295 Kennedy Memorial Drive
Waterville, ME   04901